VIA Folios 120

# The Hunger Saint

# The Hunger Saint

Olivia Kate Cerrone

BORDIGHERA PRESS

Library of Congress Control Number: 2017932219

Cover Art:
Renato Guttuso, *La Zolfara*, 1953
olio su tela, 201,5 x 311 cm
Museo d'Arte Moderna Mario Rimoldi
Regole d'Ampezzo - Cortina d'Ampezzo

Printed in the United States.

Published by
BORDIGHERA PRESS
John D. Calandra Italian American Institute
25 West 43rd Street, 17th Floor
New York, NY 10036

VIA FOLIOS 120
ISBN 978-1-59954-106-8

For my father, Peter J. Cerrone

*Sulfur was once considered one of the world's premier energy sources. The sulfur mining industry in Sicily lasted for hundreds of years until its demise in the 1980s.*

*Severe poverty and unenforced labor laws led countless Sicilian families to put their children (some as young as six years old) to work in the sulfur mines, where they experienced horrific working conditions. These children were known as the* carusi.

*Sicily, 1948*

The miners draped a soiled loincloth over the face of old Misciu and continued to work. No one was allowed to move the body until the shift's end. Ntoni adjusted the heavy basket of ore between his shoulder blades as he passed Misciu's pit. If he peered close enough inside, he could make out the figure, half-concealed in the shadows. Others appeared indifferent as they clawed at the subterranean walls with their mattocks and picks. An unending clink and scrape echoed through the tunnels. Ntoni moved ahead, eager to return outside where the air was breathable, not thick with heat and dust. He crouched beneath low ceilings, once more imagining purgatory. Perhaps Misciu's ghost had gone the same way as Ntoni's father — trapped in the farthest reaches of the mine. Tonight, he'd try to discover them both.

He took his place in line with the other boys, who climbed a long staircase of earthen steps, formed in zig-zags to help balance the shouldered weight. An arched doorway stood at the top, emitting bright outside light. From there, they'd transport the minerals to the *calcaroni*, the fat stone furnaces where the sulfur rocks were melted and refined. Underground, the stairs felt cool beneath his feet. His soles were thick and crusted over with dirt, numb to the pebbles and hard rocks that once pinched and scraped him. He bent his head further to accommodate the ore basket between shoulders. Its weight bowed him over, forcing his neck into a slight twist. There was no getting used to it, even after a month of transporting countless loads. His slow, dragging steps failed to match the steady, dogged pace of the other boys.

Together on the stairs, they formed a slow-moving cloud of shared, fleeting intimacies — the pungent whiff of body odors, the grunts and moans that escaped their lips between bits of passing conversation. Everyone had something to say about Misciu. Rumor was that he'd spent his entire life underground with no family in town to visit each Sunday, when the miners were allowed a day off. It was bound to happen here.

How long would it take to remove the body? Misciu's soul hung in purgatory like Ntoni's father's. Perhaps Saint Calogero might give some sign on his behalf too. Ntoni imagined Misciu's ghost watching them from the mine's ceiling, still trapped in his pit beneath the earth. Priests never visited the miners to administer last rites. The men worked too deep underground, some as far as six hundred feet, where the tunnels became hot like ovens, forcing them to wear loincloths and thin caps made of linen and soft canvas. Some wore nothing at all.

Another boy pushed Ntoni from behind.

"Wake up, *pazzu*. You're too slow," he said.

Crazy was the name they'd given him. He'd made the mistake of praying aloud, muttering to himself like the broken drifters who passed through Raccolto begging, displaced by the war. Someone might tear up his Saint Calogero prayer card for fun. The others worked with better efficiency. Why couldn't he be more like them? He tried to move faster. Malpelo marched ahead of him in line, imitating Misciu's choking.

"Eck, eck, eck," he said.

Everyone tried to listen. He was a bit older than the other *carusi*, and knew a *grisù* poisoning when he heard one. If the gas seeped into Misciu's pit, tainting the air around him, then it was possible that the rest of the mine was not only contaminated but on the verge of an explosion. It didn't take much to ignite firedamp. Even smoking underground was forbidden. Still, someone would have to test Misciu's pit to be sure, Malpelo explained. There was no doctor on site to examine the body, no way to sense the gas until it was too late. Perhaps they were already inhaling fresh poison.

Ntoni's lungs ached as he tried not to breathe.

It'd been an accident with one of the acetone lamps that killed his father almost a year ago. He'd spent the entirety of his life mining, right through the Second World War, until that day the men arrived at their house in Raccolto with their mule-driven carts. Ntoni's mother knew everything at first sight, even before they carried his father inside — delirious, the entirety of him covered in blood and soot.

3

"*A pezzi*," she'd said. They brought him back in pieces.

Ntoni still didn't understand all of the details surrounding the explosion, though he'd asked other miners about what they knew. He reimagined each detail like a montage of stills taken from a newsreel. His father appeared in each scene, working among the other miners until a fallen lamp splashed acetone into the fume-soaked air. Then the fires, the fallen ceiling and collapsed tunnels. Ntoni's father was pulled alive from the rubble, but not without having his legs crushed first.

Someone behind Ntoni pushed against him hard, impatient to reach the outside. He struggled to move faster and stumbled into Malpelo, knocking over both of their baskets. Panic brightened the eyes of the boys behind them, and they were quick to continue, sidestepping the fallen rubble and maneuvering up the steps, away from the scene.

"*Idiota!*" Malpelo yelled. He picked up his basket and hurried downstairs to tell the miner he assisted, no doubt. Sciavelli, Ntoni's own *picconiero*, would not be pleased if he found out. Mistakes were for the feeble-minded, the ones deserving of punishment. Ntoni crouched along the wall, his body sore. His eyes brimmed. Before him rested the small prayer card of Saint Calogero. He shot a hand over the Hunger Saint, then pushed himself up and made the sign of the cross. He brought the saint to his lips before fitting the card back into the folds of his loincloth. His sulfur rocks lay scattered in the surrounding pools of gray light. The thought of recovering them all was exhausting. But to do otherwise would mean a beating from Sciavelli. Perhaps he'd even singe his legs with one of the lanterns. It happened to others. Ntoni retrieved the basket and began loading the rubble back, piece by piece, as *carusi* moved around him. Seven years. His mother had agreed to this bargain of time not long after his father's passing. She signed Ntoni over to the Miniera Cozzo Disi mines to work off the *soccorso morto*, a loan given to his family on the promise of his labor. The mine assigned him to assist Sciavelli. Ntoni had already turned twelve that spring. Legal enough to work.

When the basket was full, Ntoni lifted it a few inches off the ground before setting it down again. The throb in his arms was immediate, almost dizzying. His nose and brow dripped with sweat; his thoughts raced in circles. There was no escaping the toil. Even if he somehow managed to escape, his family would still be stuck paying off the loan. His younger brother would also be blacklisted from working in any Sicilian mine when he came of age. Only in death could the *soccorso morto* debt be forgiven. Ntoni breathed hard, stifling the impulse to moan. Then he reached for the basket and secured it between his shoulder blades, feeling again the bite of its rough bottom ridge as a white-hot pain shot down the length of his spine.

Through the arched doorway, Ntoni reached the surface. Dozens of workers passed before his eyes, some pushing half-ton carts full of rocks along the two-by-four tracks that wound around the camp and led to the *calcaroni*. The steady purr of machines strung together the drone of voices, punctured by an occasional, indecipherable shout. Charcoal veins of smoke filled the air with rot. Built into the earth were shafts with stairways where *carusi* and miners emerged and descended.

The *calcaroni* lined the sloping basin of the camp. They stood in rows, appearing like wide triangular stone huts capped with tall, burning domes. Great plumes of bright yellow smoke wafted up from the open-air furnaces, forming clouds thick enough to obscure the sun. A rolling terrain of rock and dirt edged in around them. Nothing grew here. At the entrance to the furnaces, men noted and weighed the *carusi's* baskets to keep account of each load processed. Once approved, Ntoni moved forward, pulling the bandana around his neck up over his nose and mouth. He raised the basket above his head and deposited the minerals into one of the unlit ovens. Working so close to the kilns made Ntoni feel as if he'd catch on fire. The sulfur had to be burned at the right temperature or else it'd turn to dust. Later, the ore would be smelted into liquid and piped out through a small opening near the base of the shack. Hundreds of *mattoni d'oro*, blocks of pure sulfur, stood against the walls, waiting to be shipped away. Ntoni rubbed the wet from his eyes, still stinging from the scorching fumes. He choked on the rancid, burning smoke that blotted out the sky in yellow sulfur clouds, and hurried away from the furnaces.

Released from the weight of his basket, Ntoni's arms became buoyant. Tension lifted from his chest. He made for Ziu Peppi's workshop nearby. The mechanic appeared in one of the shop windows, turning a screwdriver into the side of some metallic thing like a crude surgeon. Ntoni waved a hand to catch the man's attention, but his friend was too absorbed in repairs to notice. Ziu Peppi adjusted the rim of his thick, square-framed glasses against his nose and parted his lips. His mouth always seemed to hang open as if too small for the mass of crowded teeth that protruded rodent-like from his gums. He didn't have the make of a miner. His build was slight, a mere extension of his overdeveloped mind, honed training as a master mechanic and translator in Mussolini's army. Ntoni sometimes heard his friend speaking French with Rosco, who ran the Miniera Cozzo Disi. Ziu Peppi's abilities were incredible and strange. Perhaps he'd also forged a special pact with the saints.

The mechanic claimed to have been a good friend of his father's, and often invited Ntoni to visit his workshop. Once, Ziu Peppi asked what he knew about France.

"Sometimes I heard about the occupation during the war. There's this café in town where you could listen to the news on their radio," Ntoni said.

"But your mother never spoke of France? Not with your father?"

"Maybe she did. They never talked about serious things in front of me."

Ziu Peppi sighed. "Of course not. But eventually you would've known. Your father had plans to mine in France. He paid me to help him leave."

"Why?"

"He wanted better for you, *piccolino*. Why else would he go?"

In this way, Ntoni learned about the service Ziu Peppi provided. For the right fee, he arranged the paperwork for

7

those illiterate miners who longed to leave Sicily for better pay abroad. Though some returned after a year or two, most never did. Ntoni couldn't imagine his mother ever approving of such plans, not with his younger brother and sister to raise.

"I kept the money for you," Ziu Peppi said. "Your father asked me to hold onto it in case something ever happened to him before he got out. He wanted the same opportunity for you. But you must be quiet about it. Don't tell anyone. The wrong set of ears could ruin everything. Rosco would have my head if he knew."

"Do you think he told my mother?"

Ziu Peppi shook his head. "Hard to say. Your father could be so quiet and stubborn. But I wouldn't tell her anything until you've made up your mind first."

Perhaps his father really had intended to abandon them. The war had broken up so many families in one way or another. Ntoni wondered this now as he stood outside of the mechanic's workshop, waving again to catch his friend's attention. Then he heard his own name called from behind. Sciavelli approached, with a loincloth tied around his waist, and sipped from a canteen bottle. Ntoni flinched.

Aboveground, the miner's skin took on a bloodless, grayish-white coloring that matched his hair and beard. The whole of Sciavelli appeared hard and swollen—muscles stretched taut along his bare arms and chest—and his shoulders, enormous rounded things, glistened with sweat and yellow sulfur dust. His fingers, thick and curved like banana peppers, curled into fists. Hands made for grasping and breaking. Sciavelli glared at Ntoni and frowned.

"Got a new job for you," he said.

They returned underground to find a handful of miners and *carusi* awaiting them before Misciu's pit. Malpelo stood at the edge of the crowd, smirking. One man held up a bronze-colored lantern, and then it became clear to Ntoni what they expected of him—to test for *grisù*. He trembled and felt his heart working inside of his chest. The miner with the lantern placed a piece of charcoal inside and dripped some water through a small fixture on top, until a few threads of smoke emerged. Adjusting the safety lamp so that a low blue flame lit, he offered it to Ntoni, who shook his head. Sciavelli frowned, impatient.

"All new miners and *carusi* need to know how it's done. I was told you weren't shown," he said, and explained how the height of the flame revealed the amount of firedamp present. If it extinguished altogether, there was more *grisù* than oxygen, and the gallery would have to be isolated off until it was safe. It wasn't hard if he never took his eyes away from the flame. Another miner assured him that the low-burning lamp wouldn't cause an explosion if there was gas inside. Ntoni doubted this. No amount of precaution could prevent the *grisù* from finding its way inside of the lamp or seeping through support beams and unearthed rock. Tunnels would continue to explode. Each month at least one miner or *caruso* perished in some way. Yet they continued to work, resigned to their proximity to death. Ntoni reached for the lantern.

9

The crowd snickered. Ntoni ignored them. He felt Saint Calogero's prayer card against his skin, and pulled his bandana up around his nose and mouth, entering Misciu's gallery. He edged forward with the safety lamp extended. With each step, he monitored himself for signs of *grisù* poisoning—a slow assault of dizziness, headache, numbness of limbs. Misciu's body remained in the corner, with the soiled loincloth draped over his face. Someone else had braved the gas enough to enter the gallery, perhaps before the threat was realized. Ntoni shuddered. He thought of his father, who appeared so small in that coffin. The strange waxy countenance of his face. Ntoni studied the lantern's small blue flame, anticipating the sudden infusion of gray or a thin extension of its tip, which would reveal the presence of *grisù*. As long as the blaze remained unaffected, they were safe. Ntoni pointed the lamp at each corner of the pit, inching deeper inside, past Misciu. The miner's pick axe still lay at an angle by his side.

A flash of movement from Misciu. Ntoni jumped. The safety lamp fell to the ground with an angry clank. Ntoni screamed and hit the floor, waiting for fire to engulf him. Laughter knifed between his ears. He looked up at the howling faces of the surrounding miners and realized that it was not Misciu stirring undead, but a mouse nestled beneath the body's cold chin, now fleeing along the cavern wall and into the darkness of the tunnels.

The men's laughter vibrated through the subterranean walls, rising to such a pitch that Ntoni wondered if they didn't intend to trigger a cave-in and have the support beams fall in around them. He stood and reached for the lantern, his face hot, studded with sweat. Sciavelli shook his head and scowled.

"You would've had us all killed," he said.

A few miners chuckled, but then the rest fell silent, hushed by Sciavelli's words. They glared at Ntoni, their faces masked in a skin of black freckles and veins of soot, as if he was the source of all the mining hazards that they'd come to know. Ntoni pushed past the men and raced ahead, knocking through the line of *carusi* on the stairs.

That night, Ntoni took a lantern and returned to the tunnels alone. He'd crept out from where he lay among the other *carusi* in their terracotta hut, and made his way through the darkness, a landscape of shadows. The grounds of the Miniera Cozzo Disi appeared endless against the dim reach of lamplight. In the cool night, he shivered in his thin cotton shirt and loincloth. His ears strained for the sound of other footsteps, fearing further torment. Still, Ntoni marched ahead, driven by a greater hunger for his father's ghost.

He reached the tall stone portal of the *discenderia*, gated now against wild dogs and foxes, and peered through its long steel bars into the ink black throat of the mine. Beyond the earthen staircase, the shaft continued like an endless drop. Ntoni squeezed through an opening in the gate and began his descent. The air chilled with dampness and he trembled hard as he reached along the dirt wall, taking his steps careful and slow, guided by touch alone. As he got deeper into the mine, a thick summer heat rose through the air. Heavy silence absorbed him. His breath alone could shatter it. This is what he hated most — the mine's fierce, unnatural silence at night, without the constant noise of machines and people. He'd already come alone here twice before. Now he held the lantern before him like a shield. A blast of intense heat greeted Ntoni as he moved deeper through the tunnels. Sweat trickled down his neck like a tiny, thousand-legged insect. When he reached the bottom of the stairway, he felt drenched and claustrophobic. He pulled off his shirt and continued onward, his free hand clasping the saint. A secret place dwelt beyond these tunnel walls, one within his reach. He understood purgatory to exist between this world and the next. The priest had said so himself.

Soon after they buried *Patri*, Father Tringali informed Ntoni and his younger siblings that their father had sent himself to purgatory. It was his own fault, the priest insisted, given the man's unwillingness to attend church each Sunday like everyone else in Raccolto. Yet Ntoni found the news hopeful. Somewhere, close by perhaps, his father's ghost waited. In the few short weeks before his mother signed the paperwork and turned him over to the mines, Ntoni devoured all that he could on purgatory from the few books kept in the basement of the church, where the children gathered for catechism lessons. The images he found depicted it as a place of suffering, one closer to Hell than Heaven, accessible perhaps through some underground passage. It was no accident that he was here in the mines now, sent to save his father.

Ntoni followed a side passage that twisted and wound its way through a maze of smaller tunnels that led deeper into the earth. One needed to crawl forward beneath the low ceilings. He shone his lantern into the caves and those tiny hollows that split off from other channels, but the light only reached so far. Ntoni felt inside of the lair, trying to decide if there was enough room to squeeze his body through. He forced himself into a womb of rock and felt the stiffness of his limbs. The boys worked in tunnels too narrow for the miners or their mule-driven carts. Perhaps they thought that *carusi* bones were bendable like mice. Ntoni tried to steady his breathing. At any moment, the walls might compress together and suffocate him. If he became stuck, the mine would swallow him whole.

Ntoni squeezed his eyes shut. He concentrated on slowing down his breathing as Sciavelli had once taught him, in order to help adjust his lungs to the heat and dust. A strange moistness hung in the air, as if the cave housed some silent living thing. Ntoni set the lantern aside. Fat streaks of *celestina*, chunks of crystallized sulfur, glittered in the walls, caught against the warm amber glow of the acetone lamp. He pulled out his prayer card and rested it near the small flickering light. He prayed for some sign of where his father's soul was imprisoned. Silence burned in his ears. He concentrated on the image of Saint Calogero, picturing him as he'd appeared in Ntoni's vision not long ago, though no one believed him when it happened. The fever made him delirious.

13

Soon after his father died, the money ran out. The funeral expenses had dried up their meager savings. Meals became slim and infrequent. Ntoni developed a taste for dirt and the remaining herbs gathered from the family garden. His mother forbade them to touch what little almonds their trees produced. Instead, she ground up the nuts, pressing out their bitterness with sugar and vanilla, and producing small blocks of marzipan to sell at the marketplace. She no longer slept. Her eyes shone wide and bright. One day, when there was nothing left to eat, she ordered Ntoni and his brother and sister outside.

Ntoni refused to obey at first. All night he'd spent awake, his body expelling waste from either end. Little worms squirmed in his diarrhea. He was too weak to stand, but that much failed to convince his mother. She wet him down with a cold rag and dressed him. He followed his brother and sister, stumbling as if in a drunken stupor. *Matri* charged ahead, clutching an empty straw basket. They soon reached the fruit and meat shops downtown. But they would not beg. They were not like the homeless drifters who loitered on street corners or slept on church steps. His mother picked through the outside trash bins with a strange display of self-possession, stopping first at the butcher's shop. She contemplated the edibility of each picked-apart bone and decaying scrap of meat, as one might judge the ripeness of a fresh blood orange. Then she used some of the discarded wax paper to wrap up her finds. Ntoni and his younger siblings watched, horrified but unable to stop her. She ignored their pleas.

A crowd soon gathered around them. Theirs was a church-going family, and it didn't take long before others took notice. At first there were only stares, but when their mother approached the rubbish bins of the congested apartment buildings nearby, the onlookers began to heckle — *cattiva madre! Brutta madre!* She became bad and ugly in their eyes. Ntoni trembled, the fever breaking over him again. Raw, itchy flames licked the insides of his buttocks. He longed to squat down and shit out his insides. His sister began to cry. One man tore the basket from his mother and emptied the trash at her feet. Perhaps they'd tear her apart like the wild dogs that roamed the countryside. They were known to strike in packs.

A robed figure moved toward them. White-bearded and tall, the saint's wizened face appeared as it did on Ntoni's prayer card. Saint Calogero, Raccolto's holy patron, once saved the town from famine long ago. Each summer, the town held a procession to celebrate its Hunger Saint. Now the crowd seemed oblivious of Calogero's presence. Ntoni met his tender gaze and collapsed.

One of the priests managed to break up the mob and escort the family home, though this much Ntoni couldn't remember. All night he convulsed with fever. A medic filled him with castor oil to flush the parasites out from his body. He slept for days, waking to find his mother, calm and sober at his bedside. She refused to believe his vision. Even Father Tringali dismissed it. He visited later that week to help arrange the appropriate paperwork for the mines. His mother followed the priest's advice without question. Ntoni should be put to work. Everyone needed to help out now, especially in these uncertain times. The priest shared news of the ongoing horrors outside of Raccolto — bands of Moroccan thieves raping and murdering their way through Southern Italy. There was no work in the surrounding cities, only rumors of devastation and chaos. Not even Palermo had begun to repair the damage caused by the air raids. People staggered about, dazed, uncertain of the new government that replaced the Fascists. But Ntoni would be one of the fortunate ones. He'd work as his father had.

"Who else is going to help us?" his mother said.

Her voice chilled him even now, deep inside of the mine. He tried again to focus on the prayer card. Low voices emerged from the distance. *Patri?* Ntoni strained his ears to listen. He maneuvered out of the cave and back through the tunnels, his movements small and quiet. Strange muffled noises echoed from a nearby pit. Ntoni peered inside.

A miner pushed himself against a boy. Ntoni froze. He didn't understand what he saw. Two nude bodies, one dwarfed by the other in size. Their movements violent and slow. The boy's face pressed against the wall, as if to merge his flesh into rock, and he whimpered. The miner squeezed a fist around the boy's thin neck. Ntoni turned and escaped back into the tunnels, his hands scratching through the dark.

Early the next morning, before the start of his shift underground, he went to Ziu Peppi's workshop. The heat was already sweltering, but inside of the small terracotta building, it was cool and shaded, a welcome respite. His friend was nowhere in sight. Ntoni leaned against one of the long workbenches and rubbed the sleep from his eyes. Already he felt more at ease. Ziu Peppi's shop was magic. The tall beams that held the studio upright appeared thin and weathered, as if the slightest storm might break it all apart. Some miners claimed that it'd stood in one form or another since Roman times. Piles of broken machinery, nails, screws and various tools littered the shelves and tabletops, their metal glittering in the sunlight like rows of silver and gemstones. On the walls hung a collection of every type of lamp, axe, drill and shovel the miners used. Each tool and contraption intrigued Ntoni, as if Ziu Peppi could build or fix anything from what lay around.

"*Ciao, piccolino!* You have something for us to add downstairs, I hope?"

The mechanic appeared from a small room in the back, carrying a steaming soup tin. His workshop housed a secret basement where he kept a cot and a large glass cabinet full of rare minerals, books, and antiques. He'd asked Ntoni to keep an eye out for any choice pieces of minerals, particularly the *celestina* stones. The slightest mention of the secret collection made Ntoni smile. Now a heaviness lodged inside of his chest. What he really wanted was to curl up in a corner somewhere and sleep.

"They had me test for *grisù* yesterday," he said.

Ziu Peppi raised an eyebrow. His lips parted, revealing the protruding tips of his crowded rodent's teeth.

"It was just a test. But we weren't really in danger," Ntoni said.

"Some test," Ziu Peppi said, and shook his head. He set the soup tin on a worktable hard, splashing some of the broth against the counter. "You want some of this, *piccolino*? You must be hungry."

Ntoni shrugged, but took the canteen and drank too fast, burning his mouth and throat with the salted taste of lentils. He had yet to get used to the mine's rigid eating schedule. Often, he chewed at the edge of his loincloth to keep the hunger-induced nausea at bay. He coughed the soup down and this triggered a series of violent sneezes.

"*Cacciastruzzu!*" Ziu Peppi said.

"*Grazie.*"

Ntoni brought his hands to his face to wipe the mucus away. A black, sticky substance webbed between his fingertips. He rubbed his hands against his bandana and sneezed again.

"*Cacciastruzzu!*" Ziu Peppi enjoyed saying the word. He erupted into his throaty chuckling. "It's all the shit you've been breathing in the mines. Not so pretty when it comes out like that, is it? Don't worry, your lungs will get used to it."

His laughed and coughed hard, then spat a wad of brown phlegm into his handkerchief and reached into his pocket for his cigarettes. Ntoni sneezed up more of the sulfur dust and grime that called his insides home, and this time spoke *cacciastruzzu* to himself. The word sounded chewed in his mouth. He handed the soup tin to Ziu Peppi, who took a few generous sips before setting it down on the worktable and resuming his cigarette.

"I don't want to work here anymore. I want to go to France," Ntoni said.

Ziu Peppi chuckled again, though his laughter was softer, more reserved. "Are you sure now? You won't be so close to Raccolto anymore. Or your friends. Your mother."

Ntoni squeezed the handle of his ore basket. Words tumbled from his lips as he tried to describe what he saw in the tunnels — the man moving against the boy, the whimpering. Ziu Peppi's face paled. An uneasy silence sat between them. Then the mechanic folded his arms and scowled.

"You should never go to the mines at night. What's wrong with you?"

"It was only because—"

Ziu Peppi waved his hand away. "I don't want to hear it. You want the same? Is that what you want?"

Ntoni shook his head and trembled.

"Then keep quiet. No one wants to hear it."

Ziu Peppi went to the center of the room, where camouflaged against the floorboards was a small wooden latch. When pulled, the little handle opened up a door to a stairway. It was the one place where Ntoni could descend and not be greeted by a dense cloud of heat. A simple room, it contained a small straw-filled cot and an open suitcase spilling over with disheveled clothing and linens, as if Ziu Peppi was ready to pack up and leave at a moment's notice. The room was well-lit by several large slow-burning lamps that were positioned around a set of glass-encased shelves facing his humble bed. Ntoni couldn't help but wonder how he'd managed to transport such display cases through the Miniera Cozzo Disi without question. Ziu Peppi loved describing his collection. Rows of rare and exquisite rocks—pyrite from the Island of Elba, green Malachite and teal apophyllite crystal from somewhere in the Orient—glittered among the little pile of white and yellow *celestina* pieces that Ntoni himself had contributed. Ziu Peppi wiped at the case with a rag until its glass appeared luminous.

"I've decided to go abroad myself soon. Maybe I'll even come with you. There's not much of a future for me here these days," he said.

Ntoni's heart lifted over the prospect of this. "What do you think Rosco will do when he finds out we're leaving?"

"For me, it won't matter. I'll still be able to collect my pension."

Many had left Raccolto to enlist for that reason. Ntoni often saw newsreels about the war in the church basement with *Patri*. Black and white shots of Italian infantrymen marching through North Africa entered his thoughts. Survival meant a pension and a life outside of the mines. His own father had not known war. Somehow he'd managed to stay underground, mining the tunnels for Mussolini's fuel. The French countryside, even what was left of it after the Germans, appeared in Ntoni's mind as a vague notion of endless green meadows. The heaviness eased from his chest.

"I wish we could leave tomorrow," he said.

Ziu Peppi chuckled low in his throat. "Sure, but these things happen when they're right, not just when we want them to happen."

"But you make them happen."

"Eventually. I have a few skills. I know the right people. God knows you can't do anything on this island without that first."

Ntoni bobbed his head. He thought of his mother, her eyes wide and desperate.

"What if I don't like it there? Maybe you could just give back what my father —"

Ziu Peppi frowned. "Give back the money? Would you really insult your father like that? After everything he did to ensure that you'd have this opportunity?"

"No, I guess not." Ntoni shrank at the mechanic's sudden anger.

"France isn't the only place. There are coal mines in America too."

After the war, the Americans passed through Raccolto in their loud trucks, unloading bags of grain and jugs of water. Ntoni was enchanted by the smiling men in their green uniforms and the strange lift and tilt of the English they spoke. Their language was much less harsh than the German he'd heard on the radio in one of the cafés in Raccolto. They greeted the children with sticks of chewing gum, one of which Ntoni saved, never tampering with its wrapper.

He spent hours studying its red letters like a code or a relic: W-R-I-G-L-E-Y-'-S.

Ziu Peppi sighed and handed Ntoni a set of working papers. Written across the top was the phrase: Mines de Lapanouse-de-Sévérac. Their destination in France. Ntoni didn't understand the language, though he recognized this phrase. It'd been painted on crates of machinery shipped to the Miniera Cozzo Disi. Still, he failed to comprehend much outside of where Ziu

Peppi told him to sign his name — a feat he'd learned in the last year alone. His reading and writing abilities remained slow but competent, which was still better than most other boys he knew in Raccolto. He signed the contracts. It was what his father would've wanted.

"Ok, *piccolino*, I want you to get a hold of your birth certificate when you go home this weekend. I'll figure out a way to have your passport made," Ziu Peppi said. He secured the paperwork back inside of his suitcase.

"They'll be looking for you," he said, and gestured toward the staircase.

When they reached the landing of the workshop, Ziu Peppi closed the trap door, his eyes darting around, as if someone might be spying on them. Before Ntoni could leave, his friend placed a meaningful grip on the boy's shoulder.

"You'll have to make some kind of arrangement with your family to pay off your *soccorso morto* loan once you're gone. Other people have sent money to their families," he said.

Ntoni nodded, his insides tensing. What would he tell his mother?

"Your father would certainly be proud of you."

"You think so? What else did he tell you about his plans?"

"In time, *piccolino*. Right now, you just keep yourself out of trouble."

Ntoni took the safety lamp and stepped back out into the dense June heat. Across from the mechanic's workshop was a small concrete hut with steel bars in the windows. A man stood inside, making notations in a fat ledger, and waved his hands at the driver of a truck parked nearby. Ntoni stopped to watch the steady, congested whir of the running engine. He never tired of seeing the trucks, no matter how often they passed. They were the only vehicles that drove through these parts on a regular basis, except once for the military convoys. The trucks delivered barrels of sulfur blocks all the way to the dockyards of Catania.

Two large men hoisted a barrel of *mattoni d'oro* between them. They lifted the drum of gold-hued sulfur bricks from a large scale and moved it up onto the back of the truck's open bed. Ntoni recognized one of them as a regular among the delivery crew. He wore a knit cap and suspenders pulled tight over his thick chest. A small grunt escaped his lips as he helped lift another barrel, holding it close like a small child before setting it down to be weighed. The barrels were packed together on the truck, though Ntoni suspected that there'd be enough room to squeeze into one of the corners. He studied the available space and tried to imagine how it might be done. The mover fit a barrel inside and gazed at Ntoni. A smile traveled between them.

Ntoni returned to the mineshafts where the steady clang of a mattock's edge rang out like metal teeth scraping bone. Most of the black shaft tower was visible from this angle; it stood upright on ribs of steel crisscrossed together beneath a hooded platform and an enormous wheel. Vast fields, the color of sawdust and ash, encircled the work site. Splintered trees and crushed rock piles studded the distant hills. Ntoni gazed long at a hedge of bramble and gnarled oleaster branches. He knew then what he'd tell his mother.

The miners returned home every Sunday, just before dawn. A small bus arrived to cart away a group of men bound for Piazza Armerina. No buses ran from the mines to Raccolto, so Ntoni walked the several miles home from the Miniera Cozzo Disi in his thin cloth shoes. The dry earth felt like a carpet of bone chips. Those who could afford it traveled by scooter; everyone else made their way on foot or by donkey-driven carts. About four or five *carusi* piled onto the back of someone's Vespa, laughing at Ntoni as they sped past.

The sun was hot against his face. It didn't feel like morning. He couldn't tell what time of day it felt like. Working underground for so long disorientated him. Ntoni moved through a valley cut high through a small mountain, its slopes honeycombed with small gaping holes—mineshafts long ago abandoned. Thin yellow grass dotted the arid dirt heaps that made up the rocky crested hills. The surrounding fields appeared thirsty, blanched of their color. Traces of smoke from the furnaces still burned through the air. A sulfurous rot clung to him. It was the one thing Ntoni's father complained about at home, how the smell and taste of sulfur lived in his skin and on his tongue. He'd soak for an hour in the large iron tub in the kitchen, while Ntoni watched from the table with his brother and sister, each in quiet awe of their father. *Matri* scrubbed off a hardened crust of grime from his body. *Patri* sat hunched over with his knees bent and drawn into his chest, as if the weight of his head was too much to hold up. Ntoni's mother reached over with a wet rag to get at his chest.

24

"Harder," he'd say. "I have sulfur chips in my skin."

Ntoni pictured them falling out like giant splinters. He figured his mother was never able to get them out but now he understood. After bathing, his father sat alone outside in the garden, where his mother planted rucola and fennel, grew almond trees, and picked dandelions to make into a soup. The children were not allowed to play during *Patri's* Sunday visits. He avoided church, though no one challenged this. On rare occasions, his father would call for Ntoni and point out the herbs and vegetables, naming each one. They stood together close. A warm, clean scent of eucalyptus radiated from his father's chest. Ntoni understood now why it was so cleansing to be away from people and noise — to smell and taste something other than sulfur. Never did *Patri* speak of the mines or whether he expected that Ntoni might work as he did. Perhaps his father had hoped for more.

Ropes of sunlight bent against the red terracotta tiled rooftops of Raccolto that emerged beyond the wide sloping hills. Ntoni approached a small cart stacked high with pomegranates. His mother's favorite. He paused before the vendor and removed one of his shoes, where inside he hid a small allowance from his earnings. Once a month, *Matri* offered him a tiny drop of the *soccorso morto* money. It never stayed with him for long. He purchased a handful of the shiny red fruit and cradled them inside of the pockets of the old trousers he wore when visiting home. A truck honked and swerved around him. Ntoni's eyes welled from the passing exhaust. The diesel fuel smelled like his future.

Ntoni's mother swept the front steps of their white stucco house, waiting for him in her long black mourning dress, the one she always wore now to church. Her dark eyes squinted hard, searching him as he approached. She crossed her arms; her lips pinched together. Ntoni crept forward and smiled as he withdrew the pomegranates.

"Are these for me?" she said. Her face brightened.

He nodded, shy always in the infrequent glow of his mother's affection. She hid the fruit into the deep pockets of her dress and returned inside.

"I have the hot water all ready for you," she said.

He followed her inside. The warmth of the small, well-lit kitchen failed to comfort him. Steam lifted from an old iron tub, reaching past the ceiling in long, translucent strips. A towel and scrub brush rested together on a chair.

"I'm going to lie down instead. My shoulders hurt," Ntoni said.

"In those dirty clothes? I just cleaned the bedsheets. Bathe first. It will relax your muscles," she said.

"Let the others go first."

"Why?" Her voice gained an edge. "You need the water hot enough to get that filth off your skin."

He imagined her scrubbing away at his father's arms and back as the old man sat hunched over, his face worn and haggard. *Patri* got the first bath each Sunday, when the water was hot and clean and fresh. Ntoni turned from the room, unwilling to take his father's place.

"I'm just too tired. Really, I don't mind going last," Ntoni said.

26

His mother slammed the scrub brush against the kitchen counter. "Lido! Come wash," she said.

Ntoni shrank along the wall as she charged past him, the gift of pomegranates forgotten. "Lido! Get in here!"

His younger brother crept from the staircase that led to the upstairs loft and pulled at a blue bandana knotted around his neck. Ntoni gave him a smile as he made for the stairs.

"You want to go up there and ruin those nice clean sheets? Fine," his mother said, her voice a shout. "But don't bother washing at all then. You can go to church and stink for all I care. Don't you dare come back down until we leave."

Ntoni shrugged, but kept his eyes downcast, unwilling to confront her stare. Upstairs, he found the loft neat and spacious—a large room where the family slept together in two separate beds—one for he and Lido, another for his sister and mother. His church suit rested atop one of the bureaus. He dressed, though it felt almost sinful to pull on fresh clothes over his dirty skin, layered in sulfur and grit. Ntoni removed the prayer card and set it upright upon the windowsill in a patch of dappled morning light. He asked Saint Calogero for forgiveness. His gaze lifted to the garden outside. He imagined his father walking across the yard with his straight-backed choppy gait.

"You embarrass me," his mother said when he returned downstairs.

Ntoni ignored her. He went to the kitchen and found a stale roll for his breakfast, then waited by the door in silence. Soon they'd be leaving. Church had a way of sedating his mother.

He'd bring up France later. Lido sat inside the tub, squeezing a fistful of soap suds into his hair. Their sister Lina, the youngest, sat nearby. She played with the old *trottola* they all once shared, making the wooden top spin against the dull floor tiles as she tugged at its string. She snuck glances at Ntoni as she always did when he returned home. Once she asked what it was like being underground in the dark for so long. Wasn't he scared?

"So ungrateful. After everything I do, you go and act this way," his mother said.

There was an order to things, an adherence to rules that he couldn't face. His brother and sister studied him, uncertain of why he misbehaved and what he'd do next to stoke their mother's rage. Soon Lina began to cry. Ntoni's mother handed Lido the towel and reeled from the kitchen.

"Don't you start now. I'll beat the living hell out of you!" she said.

Lina sobbed harder. Ntoni went to his knees and brayed like a donkey. He crawled over to his sister, nudging her knee with his forehead and pawed at the floor with his hand. It was a game *Patri* once played with them when Ntoni and his siblings were all still young enough to be held and soothed by their parents. She sniffled but managed a smile and climbed atop of him, wrapping her arms around his neck. He bounced her about until she laughed.

"You're going to ruin the knees of your good pants," his mother said, but she was calmer now, no longer screaming.

They walked the short distance to church. *Matri* led the family. A black lace veil draped over her head and face, half-obscuring her features. The *Chiesa Madre*, Raccolto's "Mother Church," towered above the surrounding gray-faced buildings. Sunlight winked against its gold-pink marble façade. Everyone from town gathered inside. The sanctuary was a wide, beautiful space adorned with stucco detail and bronze-framed fresco paintings depicting the crucifixion of Christ. Ntoni sat beside his mother in one of the pews. The church was clean and spacious in a way that their own home would never be. Numerous chandeliers hung from the high ceilings, their candlelight reflected in rows of tall stained glass windows, where images of saints basked in bright jewel tones. Bouquets of yellow and white carnations decorated the pulpit. A blanket full of bread and oranges lay before a towering statue of the Madonna with Child.

Ntoni studied the offerings, his stomach rumbling.

Father Tringali soon appeared in his regal silk cassock. His words passed through Ntoni's mind like thin smoke, failing to connect with the life he knew underground. Did the priest know about how they treated the *carusi*? Was his mother told? She sat at the end of their pew, with his siblings between them, as if she was too embarrassed to sit next to him. Countless miners and *carusi* from the Miniera Cozzo Disi sat among their families in other rows, and each looked cleaned up and presentable, with little trace of the mines in their dress or person.

His mind returned to that boy in the tunnel, pinned beneath the miner. Ntoni squeezed his eyes shut and tried again to listen to the sermon. He wondered how he might still receive messages from Saint Calogero without searching underground at night. Ntoni squirmed against the hard, wooden edge of the pew. A dull ache persisted through his limbs. His mother bent her head forward and closed her eyes as her lips intoned a soundless prayer. Through the black lace veil, she seemed tender in her devotion. He ached for this part of her. His eyes moistened. Not since they brought his father home after the accident that day did she cry. She was no stranger to death, having lost both of her brothers to the war. He swallowed hard, forcing himself still and composed. When she opened her eyes again, her gaze fixed upon the priest.

His mother's friends, other miners' wives, joined them on the walk home. *Matri* remained pleasant but distant, unable to completely relax in their company. They'd forgiven her somehow for the spectacle she'd made of herself and the family. Perhaps they attributed such behavior to grief though Ntoni remembered their disgusted faces in the crowd, soaking up the image of his mother picking through the trash. Now they smiled at Ntoni's family as if the incident had never occurred. Raccolto was a small town, too small not to be woven back into the threads of gossip and scrutiny that the others tangled around one another. Their family couldn't afford much privacy. His mother had never integrated well into Raccolto society. Her family was Catania-born, a clan of fishermen, who disapproved of her choice to marry *Patri* and move away so far inland. Ntoni had never met those relatives. No one had contacted them when his father died.

"He works so hard, this one, doesn't he? The man of the house," one of his mother's friends said. The others nodded and smiled. Ntoni looked away. His siblings walked ahead of the adults, immersed in conversation with their friends. It would look strange if Ntoni joined them, though he longed to hear what made them smile and talk with such excitement. Lido broke off into a run, laughing as he chased another boy down the street. Others followed. Perhaps they were headed to play soccer or *lupo delle ore*, a game Ntoni loved. One of them would be the wolf, standing with his or her back to the group as the rest inched closer, asking for the time — *lupo che ore sono?* For each turn, the wolf called out a number and the children took another step forward until the wolf decided they were within easy reach and shout, "*ho fame!*" Who'd be the wolf today, catching the others before they reached safety?

They entered Via Atenea, the marketplace, flooded with people after church. Ntoni recognized other miners in the street, surrounded by family. They looked so different in their good Sunday clothes — the pressed trousers and clean white shirts gave them a fresh, dignified presence. Some stood in small groups outside of the cafés, laughing and talking with friends. The men lived in Sundays.

Ntoni sidestepped fish peddlers, textile merchants, and fruit vendors, who waited by their crowded carts, shouting prices. A bakery stood beside a small macaroni factory, sugaring the air with warm scents. His stomach pinched. A butcher yelled something about fresh skinned chicken. Behind him was a little

31

shop where the flanks of animals hung from hooks out front. Several young boys, the butcher's sons, worked inside of the shop, slicing up cuts of various meats and displaying them on trays of ice. He caught up to his mother's friends.

"Now she's stopped eating. Maybe for good," one said.

One of the miner's wives had become withdrawn after her son was lost in a tunnel collapse less than a month ago, in a distant part of the Miniera Cozzo Disi. Ntoni didn't know the boy but his death still made him shiver.

"She'll make another," his mother said.

Ntoni winced. Her words gutted him.

He found *Matri* in the garden later that afternoon. The fat bushels of rucola and yellow flower heads of fennel grew in wild clumps. They continued to thrive, well after *Patri*. Ntoni knew that his mother kept up the garden as an act of devotion. She squatted low to the ground, her hands working around a sprig of parsley, jerking out the weeds by their roots. Her fingers were fast and methodical, the nails thick with dirt. When Ntoni came close enough, she looked up and smiled.

"You didn't eat much at lunch. I hope you're feeling well," she said.

His head bobbed, uncertain of how to respond.

"Let's sit in the shade," she said.

They gathered around a small table beneath one of the almond trees, its branches heavy with fruit. The plump golden husks would soon shrivel and harden, transforming into nuts.

Ntoni removed his shoes and sunk his feet into the dew-laden grass. His mother withdrew the pomegranates from her deep pockets.

"Our little treat," she said.

The fruit reminded him of the small animal hearts set aside at the butcher's shop, among the other unwanted organs, the brains and tongues sold at a discounted price. He watched his mother's hands, her skin puckered and worn. His mother took one of the pomegranates, pressing into it with her thumbs, and tore it open. Juice squirted everywhere, staining her dress, and a bit flicked onto Ntoni. She didn't seem to mind the mess she made.

"Here. It will ease your stomach," she said, handing Ntoni a slice. She waited until he ate the first seed.

Thick rows of red gels lined the inside of the skin. He plucked one off and placed it against his tongue, savoring the burst of ripe sweetness. His mother bit into a thick piece, her teeth gnashing against seeds. Bright ruby splotches stained her lips and chin as she devoured the pomegranate. She wiped some juice away and smiled at Ntoni. Her features became soft and relaxed. This warmed him. It was not an expression she wore often.

"Sciavelli must be pleased with you. You work so hard for us," she said.

He nodded and met her contented gaze, his stare lingering. Would there ever be a right time to tell her? Her smiled broadened and this much gave him courage.

"One of *Patri*'s friends has asked me to become his assistant," he said.

33

His mother squinted hard. "Another miner?"

"Ziu Peppi is the chief mechanic," Ntoni said. He heard his own voice grow distant as he explained the opportunity at the Miniera Cozzo Disi's sister company in France. But before he could explain *Patri*'s connection, his mother raised a hand to silence him. Her gaze became abstracted, her eyes deepening with new understanding, and she frowned, her lips pursing together into a bitter knot. Ntoni's voice trailed off, failing him. For a long while, neither spoke. Playful shouts from his siblings and the neighborhood children could be heard in the streets nearby. His mother finished the pomegranate and set the ravaged peels aside. Then she aimed the black stones of her eyes on him again.

"Does Rosco know about this?" Her voice was low and serious.

"Well, Ziu Peppi said he'd get—"

"I'm not asking about him."

Ntoni shook his head and looked away. A small lizard climbed along one of the walls of their white stucco house, its movements skittish and free.

"You know as well as I that Rosco won't let you go until the *soccorso morto* is paid off," she said.

"But I will pay it."

"You didn't sign anything yet, did you? Tell me you didn't sign any papers."

He channeled his father's calm and met her unwavering stare.

"What about your brother? Have you thought about how Lido will be affected? Do you really think Rosco would hire him

34

if you leave? After all of the hard work your father did to build our family's reputation," she said.

"Lido could work at Floristella Grottacalda," Ntoni said.

"When? When he's sixteen? No one but Rosco hires before that age anymore. That's another six years. What are we supposed to do until then?"

"But I'll keep working."

His mother scoffed at this. "Sure, you'll keep working. For yourself. Not for us. What do you care about what happens to us?"

She curled a hand around the barren pomegranate skins and squeezed. Her fist became white, bloodless, as if she might just mash the tough rinds into pulp. Ntoni opened his mouth to speak but found himself unable to describe what it was really like working so deep underground week after week, climbing through the tunnels with the constant anticipation of a cave-in or a *grisù* poisoning. How could he begin to describe the bruises and aches along his limbs or the way he found it harder to breath with the sulfur dust embedded deep within his throat? Miners beat *carusi* while others laughed. Didn't she know of these conditions through his father?

"Do you honestly think *Patri* would leave us like this?" she said.

Ntoni froze. Didn't she already know? Perhaps his father really had planned to abandon them after all. He tried to tell her what he'd learned from Ziu Peppi but his mother rose from the table, uninterested in his response.

Inside the house, *Matri* resumed her chores. Ntoni's sister washed laundry and wiped the countertops with rags, following their mother's orders without question. She opened all of the windows and a hot, unforgiving breeze entered, bringing with it a new layer of dust to settle upon the cleaned spaces. Ntoni lingered in his mother's presence, waiting dumbly for his own set of commands, but instead she ignored him. She moved through the kitchen in a fervent rush, feeding the stove new chunks of wood and branches as a pot of water boiled in preparation for dinner. Then she took up her broom. Never did she stop working. He sat for a moment, perhaps too close to where she needed to sweep, and then she smacked the broom handle against the side of his face.

Ntoni yelped, then squeezed his mouth shut, forcing back tears that were hot and immediate. He tasted blood.

"What? You don't want me to do my work?" his mother said.

He moved to the far side of the room, bewildered. She glared back, a stark, almost savage look distorting her features. Then she resumed sweeping. She gathered up all of the dust and grime that filled the cracks and corners of the house with such devoted intensity, as if more filth wouldn't be waiting for her to clean up the next day. Ntoni leaned against the cool wall, mute. His mother continued to sweep.

Ziu Peppi believed that most things could be fixed. He invited Ntoni to his workshop the next day, after the boy had finished his toil underground. Together they dismantled faulty

36

rock drills, pulling dull bits out of chucks. They examined the inner mechanism of each part from stem to bit, reassembling what appeared to be broken or malformed from overuse. Ntoni devoured each morsel of information he learned, certain that the knowledge would ensure his transition into the apprenticeship. Perhaps his mother might forgive him once she began receiving more money.

"What happened to your hands?" Ziu Peppi said.

Ntoni glanced at his yellow-tinted, chapped skin, which pulled taut at his bones, as if it'd shrunk. He opened and closed his hands, stretching the rough flesh. He'd become accustomed to the burning, tingling sensation that working with sulfur resulted in and didn't see the sense in complaining about it.

"A mechanic is nothing without his hands. Wear some gloves," Ziu Peppi said.

"I tried to but they get in the way whenever I carry my basket," Ntoni said.

Ziu Peppi shook his head in disapproval. He reached into one of his cabinets and withdrew a small jar of soothing balm.

"When I was your age, I worked in the salt mines of Enna," he said and spooned a dollop of the waxy substance along Ntoni's knuckles. "After a while, my hands became so numb from working with all of that salt that I couldn't feel anything. I thought I'd lose both of them."

Ntoni massaged the ointment into his skin. A tall crate box stood close to where he stood. The new drill had arrived from America earlier that day, and its journey struck him as magic.

Outside, the rains continued. The week-long deluge was unusual, and for brief intervals even halted the work of the miners with the threat of flooding. An odious creaking emerged from the roof under the assault of the downpour. It distracted Ntoni, though Ziu Peppi remained too absorbed in his work to notice.

One afternoon, the skies cleared, and the miners decided to break for lunch aboveground. The boys avoided him. Ntoni knew they didn't like him because of Malpelo. Perhaps they thought his friendship with Ziu Peppi was strange. Standing outside without their baskets, Ntoni saw how the mine left its mark on the boys. Some of the older *carusi*, the ones who'd worked in the cramped tunnels the longest, couldn't stand up straight. Their spines curved into permanent hunches. Even Malpelo's chest appeared large and deformed, his left rib cage protruding at an unnatural angle. Ntoni wondered when his own body would twist out of place.

He ate his lunch alone by a large stream that cut through the back of the mine. A thick hedge of jasmine grew along the water, its faint perfume lost in the dank, rotten air. Rosco powered a small winery here that he ran in conjunction with the mines, using the sulfur as a pesticide. Ntoni sat alone in a shaded portion of dry grass. He pressed his back up against the cool stucco wall of the distillery. Clusters of agave and prickly pears grew alongside the building. Gentle sunlight played through the swaying canopy of leaves. Low hills stretched into the distance, shining like ochre and fire. Gray clouds lazed overhead, pools of dim light forming beneath. Ntoni withdrew his *muffuletta* sandwich, given out to the *carusi* at lunch, and tried to eat, though he had no appetite. The dry, salted meat stung his torn mouth, reminding him of his mother's violence. He continued to chew and swallow. Food stuck at the back of his throat and when he raised his canteen to his lips, he felt dizzy. There was no escaping the mines—his mother, the other *carusi* and miners, would punish him at every turn if he tried to escape. Ntoni closed his eyes and focused on his breathing as if he was still weaving his way through the tunnels, desperate to return aboveground.

The grass rustled nearby, rousing him. A mouse edged closer, lured by the presence of food. The animals had lived among the men for so long that their fear was forgotten. Ntoni tore off a bit of his *muffuletta* and held it out. Mice were invaluable to the miners, alerting them of an oncoming cave-in with their keen senses. They could detect the slightest trembling in the earthen walls, long before it reached human perception. A skittish mouse was a sure sign of doom. Drilling underground required both miners and *carusi* alike to be attuned for that dreaded rumble. Then they'd have only moments to escape the underground before everything collapsed.

He kept his hand still and waited. The mouse paused, twitching its nose. Then it crept onto his hands, its tiny claws pinching against his fingertips and palm, and began to nibble. With careful ease, he scooped the mouse up in his hands and held it beneath his chin. The creature didn't resist him, though its fragile body of chestnut fur and pink skin shivered in his grasp. Its tiny heart raced. Ntoni savored the mouse's delicate touch, its tender warmth. He rested it against his chest, along with the remains of the sandwich, which the mouse began to eat.

"What's that you've got there?"

Malpelo, followed by a few others, surrounded Ntoni. Their faces appeared yellow, stained by sulfur dust. Ntoni placed the mouse in the grass. It disappeared through the thick blades before the other boys could grab it.

"Now, *pazzu* is playing with the mice."

A quick snap of laughter circled around Ntoni. He rose to his feet, his face burning. Malpelo moved a hand through the tangle of his red hair and stepped closer.

"You're pathetic," he said. A bit of spittle flicked from between his small brown-stained teeth. "They only let you work here because they feel bad for you. Because of what happened to your father—"

Ntoni tried to push past them but Malpelo blocked his path. A trace of rank meat lived on his breath.

"You're stupid enough to end up like him," he said.

Ntoni lunged forward, his knuckles making contact against Malpelo's cheek, hard enough to send the boy staggering backwards. The others hooted in surprise and delight.

Malpelo touched the corner of his mouth where his lip bled. He grinned and swung his fists hard. Ntoni dodged the blow and pushed back. The fight unhinged something ugly within him, his rage at last finding its articulation. His fists went wild, thrusting through the air until making contact with Malpelo's

40

stomach, forcing the boy to his knees. Ntoni stepped back, a bit dizzy, his head throbbing. An immediate hush descended over the others.

"What the hell are you little bastards doing over there?"

A small group of miners approached. The *carusi* scrabbled away, leaving Malpelo and Ntoni behind. Malpelo struggled to his feet, wheezing.

"Let's go now," one of the men said. "Hurry up!"

Ntoni followed in silence. He wiped blood from his lips and studied the dirt and gravel-studded path that led back to the furnaces. A light rain began to fall.

They joined a small group of men on the platform, waiting beneath the steel awning of the elevator tower. Ntoni stood apart from Malpelo; the boys ignored one another. The miners gossiped about a possible *grisù* contamination in a new tunnel, and the ongoing threat of Rosco reducing their pay. Flies swarmed around Ntoni's head. There were too many. The grime and sweat of the men attracted them like mad. Ntoni swatted at the air but the flies continued to land on his skin and hum quick, desperate phrases in his ears. What punishment awaited?

He squeezed between eight miners inside of the elevator, and the cage door slammed shut. In the immediate, slow descent, the tiny box flooded with darkness. Ntoni pressed against the others and held his breath. The service elevator was prone to accidents. For a moment, he imagined its cables snapping and falling through the earth. A lamplight shone, held up by one of the miners, and wove threads of gray light across their features. Ntoni clenched his teeth as he braced himself for their landing.

A man began to sing, "*Santa Barbaredda, affacciata a la finestredda,*" and was soon joined by the others, "*carmàti 'sta timpesta; mannàtila unni 'un cc'è suli.*" Their voices harmonized together into a string of diminished chords: "*unni 'un cc'è luna, unni 'un cc'è nissuna criatura.*" It was the prayer for Santa Barbara, the patron saint of miners. She watched over them from a celestial window and they pleaded with her to calm the storm in their lives, drive it past the sun and moon, far from any living creature.

The elevator reached the ground with a sudden, violent jolt. Ntoni felt his legs weaken, half relieved to find himself still intact. The doors pulled apart, scattering the voices. The miners filed out into the mouth of a somber-lit cave. Several lamps hung fixed along the walls of its long throat, cut through rock and bolstered up by thick wooden beams. A thick, airless heat, the breath of the underworld, greeted them, bringing with it traces of urine and sweat. No one seemed to notice the stench though Ntoni forced himself not to gag. The boys waited as one of the men left to retrieve the miners they assisted. Malpelo began to wheeze and cough. His face looked ashen in the lamplight. Ntoni removed the canteen from around his waist and extended the bottle to Malpelo.

"Here."

Malpelo took the water and drank long, without looking up. After a moment, he began to choke again, then brushed a hand across his mouth and handed Ntoni back the small jug.

"Thanks."

Sciavelli emerged from one of the tunnels that funneled into the entrance of the pit. Shadows hugged the sides of his sharp nose and chin in menacing stripes. He stood under the lamplight, glowering at the boys, as if they'd disrupted him out of a long and angry slumber. Behind him appeared Malpelo's miner. Each man wore a freckle of blue scars across his nose and a veined forehead from various cuts and scrapes that had become tainted by sulfur air–the skin permanently stained.

"I've been told you boys like to settle your problems on the Miniera Cozzo Disi's time. I wonder how Rosco might feel about that," Sciavelli said.

"We'll have to have a talk with him," the other miner said.

"Perhaps there's a way we could teach these two a thing about working together."

"That could be arranged."

Neither boy responded. Their miners exchanged parting glances and nodded. Something treacherous was decided. Ntoni turned away from Malpelo and followed Sciavelli through one of the tunnels. Dim lantern light drew thick shadows across the long crooked passage. Metal pierced rock, again and again. Clink and scrape. The occasional drill hummed, burrowing deeper into the walls as minerals fell to the ground in chunks. Scattered human voices surfaced above the mechanical clamor, devoid of meaning. Each noise carried an inescapable echo that droned on inside of Ntoni, dictating the rhythm of his own movements as he passed through the tunnels. A strange heat emitted from the walls, as if tiny, smoldering fires lived inside each rock.

Then the passageway emptied into a wide pit that offered little release from the heat. Sciavelli set the lamp on a wall hook and, removing his pants, tied a loin cloth around his midsection. Ntoni did likewise, then crouched down and began to load his ore basket. A long stretch of *celestina* glowed in the wall. Sciavelli swung his pickaxe, spraying black splinters into the air. No words were exchanged between them as they worked. They seldom ever spoke, unless Sciavelli was giving instruction or criticism. Ntoni heaved the basket up against his neck.

He passed the ventilation shaft built into the wall just outside of Sciavelli's pit. He couldn't help but think of his father, as if *Patri*'s ghost clung to the ladder attached to the shaft, leading aboveground—an escape route used in the event of a cave-in. Ntoni paused for a moment, balancing his basket with one hand, and reached over to touch the last rail of the ladder. It was made of leather and rope. Most ventilation shafts contained them. Perhaps if only his father had moved faster, he could've pulled himself up along the rope and through the shaft to safety. Ntoni readjusted the basket and continued moving—the weight of the sulfur rocks against his shoulders became intolerable if he remained still for too long.

At certain points, the ceiling came down so low that the only way forward was to scrape along the gravel floor on elbows and knees. What further punishment awaited him? Perhaps they'd extend the terms of the *soccorso morto* loan. It was known to happen. Some old men had stayed *carusi* for life. Their growth appeared stunted from endless tunnel crawls, their shoulders and backs scooped like question marks. The adult *carusi* sometimes appeared among the boys, but everyone avoided them. These men frightened Ntoni too, though he couldn't help but gawk at their disfigured bodies and eerie stoicism, as if the capacity for expression had been beaten out of them.

He joined the *carusi* at the stairs leading to the surface. Ntoni kept his bandana over his nose as he passed the others. Still, dust coated the inside of his mouth and nostrils, leaving his throat scratchy and raw. Around him, other boys wheezed — *ack, ack, ack* — their lungs clogged with residue. Nearby, the miners grunted with each heave of their arms — their axe or shovel a mere extension of their bodies.

Aboveground — a vast and brilliant sky. The rain had cleared, leaving the hot sun in its wake. Ntoni craned his head to steal glimpses of it as he moved toward the furnaces. He wondered if it wasn't unlike the boundless sea, which he'd never had the opportunity to visit. Somehow, he'd transform himself into a bird and never again feel the hot sulfur dust imprison him, inside and out.

A loud, violent explosion broke apart his thoughts. Ntoni rested the basket of rocks at his feet. He pulled the bandana from his face and wiped away sweat. Others halted and looked at one another, their eyes wide and questioning. Perhaps there'd been a cave-in or one of the furnaces imploded. Then a miner raced past, calling for help. The news came in shouted fragments. Ziu

Peppi's workshop. Roof collapsed. Ntoni abandoned his sulfur basket and hurried forward.

Only the stone walls remained intact, cradling the debris. Broken chips of rust-colored terracotta tiles and the split ends of wooden beams scattered among the collection of mining tools and machines parts, blanketing the area in complete disarray. Ziu Peppi remained trapped underneath. A dozen or so men pulled apart the wreckage, tossing aside handfuls of rubble in their search as they hollered to one another. Ntoni worked among them, his hands clawing through bits and shards. He caught only some of their words, how the rainstorms had weakened the roof beams. Didn't the mechanic suspect anything wrong? He'd spent so much time there. Ntoni tore at the rubble. Tiny splinters pinched along his fingers. If Ziu Peppi wasn't dead perhaps his wounds had left him maimed. They'd amputate his limbs. Ntoni blinked back tears. Then he remembered the hidden cellar and directed a few of the men to dig in that spot. They soon cleared away the entrance point, uncovering part of a staircase that led into darkness. A voice cried out to them. The men shouted as they entered, soon emerging with Ziu Peppi, bloodied but whole and alive.

They carried the mechanic back a little ways from the building, where he could only sit up. He stared open-mouthed and silent at what was once his workshop. Ntoni stood over him, whispering his name, but his friend remained oblivious.

46

"He saved his own life being down there," one of the miners said.

Ntoni turned and saw that Rosco had come out to inspect the destruction. His was a presence that demanded everyone's immediate attention. He waddled through the crowd on his short, chubby legs and wiped a handkerchief against his thick neck.

"Where is my drill?" the *padrone* said.

The American tool was irreplaceable. Rosco commanded all of the men to find it. Ntoni crouched beside Ziu Peppi, who also tried join them, but not for the drill. He knew that what really concerned the mechanic was the security of his secret possessions, his passport and the working papers that held the keys to their next lives. But when his friend tried to rise, pain overwhelmed him, and he was forced back to the ground. Rosco glared at the fallen man with disgust, as if Ziu Peppi himself had something to do with the accident. He ordered that the mechanic be taken to his office where he'd find a doctor to treat him.

"I'll visit soon," Ntoni said.

Ziu Peppi ignored him. Rosco stood close by, watching as the miners unearthed his American drill, still encased in its tall crate box. He offered Ntoni a handful of black fish-shaped licorice drops made from a factory in Calabria. Flecks of lint stuck to the candies, along with a black ringlet from his head or elsewhere.

"No thanks," Ntoni said.

He returned to where he'd left Sciavelli's ore and discovered that the basket was gone. His heart beat high in his chest. Ntoni didn't bother to ask the others for help. Someone had made off with it as a cruel joke, or perhaps in all of the confusion, it'd been picked up by mistake. Ntoni returned underground and found the miner still at work. Sciavelli threw down his pickaxe and swiped a thumb under his nose, removing a layer of sweat and grime.

"Where have you been?" he said.

"There was an accident at the mechanic's shop. Rosco wanted everyone to help clean up the rubble," Ntoni said.

Sciavelli nodded; any reference to the *padrone* being involved was enough to dismiss most wrongdoings, but he still frowned at Ntoni.

"Where's your basket?"

Ntoni shook his head. He knew it didn't matter how he tried to justify the loss; Sciavelli would never forgive him for it.

"Answer me."

"Someone took it."

Sciavelli's features hardened. He scrunched his heavy brow together, unable for a moment to believe it. This was the most severe rule that a miner's assistant could break.

"Why would you leave my sulfur unattended?"

"I had to help. Ziu Peppi's workshop collapsed."

Sciavelli turned away without response. In a corner by some mining tools rested a sack that could also be used to carry the rubble. It wasn't as sturdy or easy to balance against his neck as the basket, but it'd have to do for now. Ntoni took the sack and bent over the pile of sulfur rocks to begin collecting the new load. Before he could reach for the first one, Sciavelli slammed him back against the wall, a savage growl rising from his throat.

"Don't you touch it!"

He tore the belt from around his waist and lashed it across Ntoni's face and chest. The leather whipped against his arms and shoulders, branding hot streaks into his skin. Then Sciavelli paused, breathless, and Ntoni bolted from the pit. He squirmed through the narrowest tunnels until reaching the stairs. Outside, he raced past the others, not stopping until he cut through the thick jasmine hedge that grew along the large stream near Rosco's winery. It was the one place that might be free of miners and *carusi* in the late afternoon. Ntoni sat along the edge of the brook, his hands trembling as he gathered cool water between his palms, pressing it against his bloodied cheeks and lips. The skin along his arms and chest blistered. He splashed water against his face and sobbed. The constant whirring hum of machinery pulsed inside of his ears. His mother and siblings would never forgive him if he deserted the mines, but how much longer could he really stay now? He needed to speak with Ziu Peppi. There was no way forward but out.

He lay awake among the other sleeping *carusi* that night. Tears wet his cheeks and earlobes. His back ached. A thin layer of straw covered the cold stone floor of the hut where all of the boys slept together. Dim portions of moonlight shone through a lone window, casting a gray film over everyone's skin. Ntoni's face and side continued to throb — the long, swollen welts raw to the touch. The others formed a living creature around him, warming the space with their bodies. Soft breath rose and fell in gentle waves of sleep, punctured by the occasional snore or fart. Privacy was a thing of luxury. Ntoni could not stretch his arms without touching another. Still, he felt so distant from everyone. A cold sensation expanded through his bones, frosting over his innards as he studied those neighboring faces, still and peaceful in their slumber. There was no one he could speak to now; no one who'd acknowledged his wounds earlier, as if the slightest presence of trouble made him invisible. He considered his mother's anger. She'd only punish him with this proof of disobedience branded across his skin.

Already they'd taken Ziu Peppi back home to Raccolto to recover. How could he get to him now? Perhaps someone was already pillaging through the fallen workshop. Ntoni gazed at the ceiling, his restless eyes searching the crisscross of the black roof beams above, their corners strewn with cobwebs. Who knew how much longer they'd hold up? Another rainstorm might send the ceiling down, crushing them all in their sleep. He climbed from the pile of boys, careful not to upset their tangle of limbs.

Outside the moon stole behind inked clouds. Some of the windows glowed from Rosco's palace, which towered in the distance, overlooking the mining grounds. The building stood more than three stories high, the size of a small factory, and fronted an enormous iron door. The *padrone* was known for giving parties there when the Miniera Cozzo Disi's owners visited from Northern Italy. Ntoni strained to listen but heard nothing but the immediate noise of crickets and mosquitoes, then the low, muffled voices of miners speaking nearby, unseen in the shadows. He moved faster through the dark, finding the path with his small acetone lantern, and soon reached the workshop. Ntoni unearthed the half-blocked stairway to Ziu Peppi's underground studio. He slipped past the obstructing debris and entered the secret room.

The roof had destroyed the display cabinets. Thick jagged shards of glass carpeted the floor, reflecting in the lamplight. Ntoni took careful steps around the sharp pile. He looked about for the suitcase, but it was gone. Already stolen. Ntoni sighed. A moth fluttered against the nape of his neck, its wings humming like a small anxious motor, and he flinched, almost dropping the lantern. The light caught on something that made him pause. He moved closer and shone the lamp upon a small rock made of shimmering beige petals. The Desert Rose. Somehow it'd survived the accident, entirely intact in all of its strange geometric perfection. Ntoni pocketed the crystal and searched for his working papers.

He approached the bed and pried through the cement and roof tiles blanketing the mattress, before discovering the suitcase fallen off to the side. Wedged between wall and box spring, it rested open, contents undisturbed, with the corner of a small beige envelope sticking up. Ntoni set the lantern down and grasped the package, tearing open its flap. Instead, he withdrew a thick stack of blue and gray-tipped bills. He blinked hard, disbelieving. Ziu Peppi's profit from the other miners. Perhaps his father's portion too. He'd never seen so much money in his life. Ntoni wondered how much *Patri* spent to have his working papers arranged. Ntoni's hands trembled over the bills, unable to count them. The others would kill one another over it if they knew. Heat wet the space above his lips. He fit the envelope beneath his shirt, then thought better of it and tied it around his waist with a piece of rope he found among the debris. The envelope pinched against his skin as he returned outside, uncertain of what to do next except to hide it.

Sciavelli explained how the dynamite would be set up along the tunnel walls. He stood before Ntoni and Malpelo, and handled one of the explosives, describing how to detonate it with an unnatural sense of calm. Ntoni couldn't bring himself to look at the man head on. The long red welts in his skin burned. It was as if the beating had never occurred—from savage to reserved, the miner became a different person altogether. Ntoni had arrived in Sciavelli's pit earlier that morning to discover another basket waiting for him. Neither spoke of the incident. The new task absorbed him: some miners had detected a *grisù* contamination nearby and after a brief discussion had chosen him and Malpelo to close off the affected tunnels as punishment for the earlier fight.

Ntoni felt Malpelo's gaze, sizing up the extent of his wounds. Their eyes met, sharing a brief look of terror. No other *caruso* had ever done such work, though there had always been rumors, especially regarding the narrowest tunnels. They followed Sciavelli to the gallery. Others paused in their work and stared at them. Everyone knew that this was not the safest way to block off *grisù* from leaking into the rest of the mine. One needed to use an air ventilator to pump out the toxic gases from the shut-off tunnel where the poison was contained. Explosives were used to form new pits and tunnels through breaking up rock and large portions of earth. It was ridiculous to use them for any other purpose. Ntoni knew this. To block off a *grisù* contamination by destroying the passage to the affected tunnel was next to insane. He'd heard other miners complain about Rosco before, always eager to save money. It was cheaper to close off the area by blowing up the immediate surrounding tunnels instead of investing in another expensive machine. Even if that much could set off a cave-in.

They reached the entrance to a wide pit that was flagged down with a strip of red cloth, the warning for *grisù*. The pit led to another tunnel that was blocked with several large planks of wood and bits of insulation. Sciavelli warned them not to open or tamper with the makeshift portal because it might expose the rest of the mine to the fumes. But they were to set up the dynamite here. If they destroyed this area, then it might slow the *grisù* or prevent it altogether from advancing. Ntoni and Malpelo wore thick rags wrapped around their knees for the low tunnel ceilings that forced them to crawl. They tightened handkerchiefs over their faces and stepped into the pit.

Inside was a shovel and a hand rock drill that rested beside a carton of dynamite. Sciavelli pried off the lid of the box and gestured to the rows of brown sticks that lined the interior. They were to carry them in their sacks, after the holes were drilled, lacing the pit and surrounding tunnels with explosives except for the one poisoned with *grisù*. Other miners would detonate the bombs later that evening, once the shift was through.

"Don't stop until the box is empty," he said.

When he left, Malpelo reached for the drill and tried to hoist it up in his arms before setting it down upright. The tool, with its long, thick stem and sharp bit, stood almost as tall as he. Long cords extended from its base and snaked out through the pit and back all the way aboveground, providing the feedline for the electricity to make the motor run, and a waterline that prevented the machine from overheating. Malpelo fit his hands along the base, turning on the drill as he tried again to lift it. The tool growled and shook hard enough to spring loose from the boy's hands, landing hard against the ground.

"Turn it off, turn it off. You want to break it?" Ntoni said.

Malpelo scrambled to cut the power. "You try it then!" he said.

Ntoni gripped the handle along its base and hoisted the drill up only a few feet before the muscles in his arms grew tired and weakened. Sweat coated his face and neck, stinging the open gashes that became raw again under the strain. The rock drill had to weigh forty or fifty pounds at least. Other miners could handle it with ease — some working the tool with only one arm. Yet for all the strength he and Malpelo had built up, carrying countless loads of sulfur, neither could handle the drill alone. Ntoni set the machine down. His sides ached; his lungs felt worn and bruised. It was difficult to breathe or even think straight in such a hot, cramped space.

"The bastard is just humiliating us. He wants to get us killed," Malpelo said.

"Well, what do you want to do then? Use a shovel?"

"We can use a pickaxe or something. There might be one in another pit."

Ntoni shook his head. He steadied the drill upright, measuring with his eyes the right angle they needed to position the bit along the tunnel wall and pierce a series of fine, exacting holes to insert the dynamite. They needed enough balance to achieve the right position. Ntoni scratched at his bandana, already damp and irritating his skin, but he didn't remove it in fear of inhaling *grisù* poison.

"We can both use the drill if we share the weight and move it from the back. I know a way how to do it. I've worked with these drills when I was training to be the mechanic's assistant," he said.

Malpelo squinted hard. "You?"

"Let's try and see what happens. I don't want to be stuck down here. Do you?"

They lifted the drill together — Malpelo clutching the handle while Ntoni squeezed his palms around the feedline and base of the stem, guiding its movement as they steadied the drill along the tunnel wall.

"Keep your hands steady or it will fly right out from us," he said.

He switched on the power. A roar escaped from deep inside the machine. The drill lurched forward and rattled with sudden life, as it tried to escape their grasp. They struggled to keep their hold against its violent trembling, but managed to position the tool against the wall and force the bit through rock. Shards of ore shot out in a cloud of smoke. Dust filled the air. Ntoni turned his face from the spray of debris, and pulled back the drill.

They took turns positioning the tool, switching places securing the base and handle or lifting and guiding the bit into place as it jackhammered through rock, forming a hole for the dynamite. The rapid back and forth motion of the drill pulsed through Ntoni's arms, making him feel as if he'd become part of the machine. Splinters of rock grazed the exposed portions of his face. His arms throbbed with fatigue. They continued working, pausing only to give direction or argue over the tool's deafening growl. Somehow, they managed to pull the drill through even the tightest spaces, and found a certain rhythm in working together as they reached the length of the tunnel, taking short breaks at intervals to rest their limbs. Ntoni worked without question, afraid that if they stopped they might lose momentum and not continue. He forced himself not to think about how the vibrations created in the rock might further endanger them. Perhaps they could even set off the explosives before they had time to set the dynamite in place. What wasn't possible?

Later they carried the explosives on their backs. Handling the dynamite unnerved Ntoni. It rested within a leather sack balanced between his shoulder blades. Lighter but more lethal than any ore he'd ever been asked to transport. He kept a few paces ahead of Malpelo, holding the lantern out before them, clearing the way through the unlit passages. Lamplight shone against the fist-sized holes they'd drilled into the walls. Soon they paused again to unload more explosives. Each stick appeared thick and sturdy enough, reaching a little longer than one of his hands, and was sheathed in a protective brown wrapping with faded red letters printed along its side. The dynamite felt solid to the touch as if it was made of wood instead of some powdered chemical encased in cardboard. They set the sticks into each opening, stringing the explosives together from their blasting caps with a long piece of electric cable. One of the miners would ignite the fuse from afar after everything was set up, and they were far away from the tunnels, safe aboveground.

"There's no way anything could explode without a lit fuse, right?" Ntoni said.

Malpelo snorted. "There wouldn't be much we could do about it if it did."

"Just be careful not to drop anything. Or bump your sack against the walls. What if they blow up?"

"Shut up, will you?"

They continued in silence.

57

Dusk greeted them when they returned aboveground. Sciavelli was gone, and neither saw the miner in charge of detonation—they were shooed away as soon as they finished the task—but as they stood outside of the large stone portal of the *discenderia*, the entrance point that the *carusi* used, they heard a great, loud blast. The earth shook with violent tremors, as if the ground threatened to swallow up the entire Miniera Cozzo Disi. Then the area was calm again; a few miners emerged from the tunnels, indifferent to any possible threat. Ntoni shuddered.

"Six more weeks. Then it's over for me," Malpelo said. He offered his cigarette. Ntoni hesitated in accepting, confused by the sudden friendliness.

"Are you going to the Floristella Grottacalda mines?" He struggled to get the words out before coughing on a few puffs. Malpelo smirked.

"Give me that," he said.

He took the smoke and placed it between his lips. Something had changed between them underground. Neither was quick to be rid of the other's presence. Ntoni walked onward. A gentle breeze curled against his cheek. The moon appeared in the twilight above.

"No, not Floristella. I'm not going to end up there either."

Ntoni smiled. They had at least that much in common. He thought of Ziu Peppi's envelope, how he'd buried it in one of the giant mounds of dry sulfur dirt in a discarded area of the Miniera Cozzo Disi, seldom used. It was too dangerous to carry around. There was no one outside of Ziu Peppi who could know about the money. On Sunday, he'd finally get to see his friend in Raccolto, where the mechanic was sent home to recuperate.

"What will you do then?" Ntoni said.

"My uncle has friends who own an olive grove outside of Enna. There's work once the harvest season begins again," Malpelo said.

"Oh?"

"They ship their olives all over the world. There are trucks that come and take away big crates of the stuff. I've seen them before. They go to the dockyards in Catania and leave from there."

An image of oceans entered Ntoni's mind, carried in the sureness of Malpelo's voice. The sea extended all around him, fitting against the horizon. Its calm ink-tipped waves alternated between hues of cerulean and indigo, as he'd seen it portrayed in various drawings from a few maps and posters hung in the cafés. He'd never visited the shoreline himself, though his mother once shared her memories of living by the Mediterranean in Catania. Her father and brothers would disappear on their boat for weeks, fishing for *tonno* and cod. Sometimes her mother and sisters would stand along the warm beaches, waiting for their arrival. Their return was never certain.

The ocean extended forever in Ntoni's thoughts, somehow reaching France and a new life. He wondered what Malpelo might do about his *soccorso morto* debt once he left the mines. Would his family pay it? What would happen if they didn't? Ntoni's chest tightened. He felt again the fatigue in his arms.

"Oh and there's this."

Malpelo took out a photograph and handed it to Ntoni. A black and white shot of a laughing girl with long dark hair.

"She's pretty."

"Do you have a girl?"

Ntoni shook his head. He imagined himself older, as a miner coming home to a wife who washed him in a steaming tub, surrounded by young children all talking at once. They were another kind of *soccorso morto*. He could never leave them. The breath caught between his lungs.

"Then I'd really be stuck here," he said.

Malpelo laughed. He smoked in thoughtful silence. Soon his features became a vague impression against the darkness—the smoldering ember of his cigarette cast a bright, intermittent glow.

Malpelo offered him a ride back to Raccolto early that Sunday morning. They sat together on a Vespa while another boy drove. It seemed crazy to ride this way. Ntoni leaned forward, his hands grasping at his friend's shirt, desperate not to fall off as they sped forward. The mine soon faded from view, then became impossible to see. A shimmer of light fanned out around the distant peaks of the wide sloping land they raced toward. His stomach knotted over what Ziu Peppi might say when he saw the envelope again, saved from the wreckage of the workshop.

Once they reached downtown, the boys made plans to meet up after church at Malpelo's house. One of the older *carusi* wanted to visit a certain prostitute who lived nearby. He sneered at Ntoni.

"You're so young, I bet you never had a girl."

The boys laughed. Ntoni smiled and shrugged, his face reddening. Women were a species apart from his mother and sister, strange and threatening. Even the neighborhood girls made him nervous. He knew the way men spoke of female bodies, their voices charged with pleasure. Still, he couldn't connect this desire to what he'd seen underground, the violence done to that boy. Who was he? Ntoni had run away before seeing the *caruso*'s face. He gazed long at the narrow cobblestone street, already bustling with merchants, as if the shopkeepers might possess the answer.

Wedged between a crowded row of low cement and stone buildings stood Ziu Peppi's house. Ntoni knocked at the door until an elderly woman dressed in a black kerchief appeared on the balcony above. Her pale shrunken hands grasped at the black railing as she peered down at him.

"What do you want?"

"I have something to tell Ziu Peppi."

The woman's brow wrinkled. "Are you from the Miniera Cozzo Disi?"

"I'm his friend."

"Well he's gone away now to Floristella Grottacalda, and it's a good thing too, after what happened. He lost everything."

Her voice trembled. She cursed him and returned inside, slamming the tall French doors behind her.

"I have something of his!" Ntoni said.

61

He pounded again at the door and was answered with silence. Soon he retreated to the street. The envelope felt heavier inside of his trouser pocket. What would he do with the money now? Would they still go to France? Ntoni's thoughts raced. When he reached home, he found the front steps deserted. His mother was inside, already in her black mourning dress as she helped prepare his siblings for church. He slipped off his thin shoes and held them between his hands.

"Is the water still hot?"

She glared at him, her lips parting with ready criticism. Then she got a good look at the welt that stretched across his face and became quiet. Her eyes smarted, but she said nothing and turned to finish buttoning up the back of Lina's dress. His sister stared hard at his face.

"Go put on your shoes," his mother said to her.

Ntoni undressed. He folded his clothes into a ball around the envelope, then stepped inside of the tepid bath, which was darkened with a film of soot from his siblings. His mother scrubbed hard against him with a wet rag, massaging his back and neck with such thorough precision that it forced the tension from his body. He became still, his resistance gone, and allowed her hands to work as she pleased, sloughing off that second, mineralized skin while he tried to make sense of Ziu Peppi's cold departure. Ntoni's mother grazed his face with the wash cloth.

"What happened?"

"I'm fine."

She paused again when nearing the raised strips of bloodied flesh along his side. Her hand became slow and gentle as she cleaned around the wounds. Ntoni's siblings stood near the tub, all talking at once — how the market sold tiny marzipan fruit, miniature replicas of oranges and pomegranates, and what the nuns taught them about St. Francis of Assisi in catechism school, and how they'd managed to trap a few doves for today's meal — the stories collided into one another, fragments competing for the little attention that Ntoni gave them. His mother shooed them away.

"Give your brother some peace!"

Lido edged closer. "Next month they let me start," he said.

Ntoni glared at him. He rose from the tub and reached for a towel hooked over the back of a chair. Then he took the dirty pile of clothes and balled them together in his fist. For a moment, he considered handing over the envelope to his mother in exchange for his brother's life.

"What about your hair? You're not finished," she said.

Ntoni ignored her and pulled on his church outfit. Lido stared at him, his round, soft features beaming for approval. He wore a dirty blue bandana around his neck, even over his good Sunday clothes. Any attempt to pry it away only induced a screaming tantrum. His dark curls grew in uneven tangles over his forehead. He dug his hands into his pockets and rested on the back of his heels the way the old men did, adrift in endless conversations, on street corners.

"You're not going to the mines. You're only ten. Not old enough," Ntoni said.

Lido scrunched his face into a bitter pout. "Why? I want to work!"

"You're too young."

His mother slammed the wash rag against a corner of the tub. "Who are you to say he's too young? We all need to help out. Rosco says there's work for him."

Ntoni turned to face her, his voice low. "You talked to Rosco about it?"

*Matri* smoothed out the wrinkles in her dress as she stood. Her long, icy gaze steadied on him until he looked away.

"He wants to help us," she said.

"You really asked if—"

Ntoni shook his head, unable to keep the rage from distorting his voice.

"I don't see what the problem is," she said. "Rosco has hired boys that young before. There are ways of working around the law. Besides, he could even assist you."

"He's too young."

"No I'm not," Lido said.

"It's dangerous. You could—"

Ntoni glanced at Lina, whose stare distracted him. He couldn't say too much about the mines, not in front of her. *Matri* forbade it. There was no way of making Lido really understand the hardships that awaited him. By the time he knew, he'd already be locked into his own *soccorso morto*.

"Why should he go now? He can finish another year of school. I can still take care of things."

His mother shot him a look. "So you're staying with us now?"

He looked away, overwhelmed, a heaviness expanding within him. *Matri* turned for the door.

"Come," she said. "We're going to be late for church."

Ntoni watched them leave. He could not follow.


The man operating the small booth at the entrance of the Miniera Cozzo Disi could offer no other information about Ziu Peppi's disappearance, only that he'd made a single attempt to retrieve his possessions, but was turned away, the workshop being too unstable with the cleanup still underway. This disheartened Ntoni. He thought to ask around that morning upon returning to the mines, hoping that Ziu Peppi had left a note for him, detailing their plans to leave Sicily together. Ntoni asked the entrance point clerk again. No one came or left without passing him first; he punched the time cards of each miner, and weighed every barrel of sulfur before it was hauled off by the trucks.

"*Nun u sacciu*," the man said. I know nothing.


Ntoni and Malpelo's success in closing off the *grisù* contamination soon invited the attention of other miners, and even Rosco himself. The *padrone* demanded that the boys be pulled from their lives as *carusi* and made to complete similar small-scale demolition and excavation gigs. They worked in tunnels that narrowed beyond the miners' reach. Each new job brought the same terrifying risk as the first, though Ntoni dared not to challenge Rosco's will. Even Sciavelli grumbled over losing his *caruso*'s assistance, but the *padrone*'s say was final. He refused to pay the boys extra for their work. Ntoni resisted complaining about this. Each night, he returned to where he'd buried Ziu Peppi's envelope and pressed the money between his fingertips. Could it repay the *soccorso morto*? His mother had never shared with him the exact value of the loan.

The demolition work demanded every bit of his focus. He felt the grit and dust of sediment and sulfur ore become as much a part of him as the vibrations of the rock drill that coursed through his hands and into the bones and joints of his small frame. Thoughts of Saint Calogero began to desert him, though one night, he longed for his father's presence and reached for the prayer card in the folds of his loincloth, only to find it gone.

The mechanic's workshop still remained in pieces. Rosco kept vague about the details surrounding its repair. Once the *padrone* passed Ntoni and Malpelo on break. He was flanked by two well-dressed strangers — inspectors sent from the mine's owners in the North to inspect the grounds and take photos of the damage. They carried cameras around their necks and took notes on what they saw.

"I could help with the cleanup," Ntoni said.

Rosco glared at him, then smiled.

"You'd be amazed by the work of these two," he said to the inspectors, and then added to Ntoni, "want your picture taken?"

He grinned at Malpelo. Few people they knew back home could afford to own a camera. They stood by the great arched mouth of a *discenderia* and posed. Ntoni flushed, self-conscious of the long scar branded across his face by Sciavelli. The marks were slow to fade. Then the camera clicked and flashed, and Rosco turned away, promising to send a copy of the photos. He moved with the inspectors toward the remains of Ziu Peppi's shop.

Countless hours of working together fostered a familiar comfort between Ntoni and Malpelo. He even invited Ntoni on their breaks to the *cimitero*—a special place, known but exclusive. One needed to be invited by another, and led through the path that wound along great mounds of abandoned sulfur dirt and uneven patches of tall yellow grass to reach the scrap yard for all of the discarded machines—the broken drills, air pumps, carts and misaligned tracks scattered among bits of wheels, tool heads, and timbers of steel heaped together, rusted and forgotten.

They came together at the *cimitero* during breaks or on stolen time, stepping back into their old selves and discarding the name *caruso* altogether. There were endless games and contests, things to be climbed over or into, pried apart and explored. They crawled through the rotted-out ends of sulfur barrels, then took turns racing down the sides of an enormous sulfur dust hill on sleds cut from smooth metal. Some of the boys made crude weapons out of broken tool heads and pretended to fight one another. Others played soccer. Here Ntoni could forget the mines and the loss of different life abroad.

Later in the week, he worked with Malpelo in the removal of an unstable pillar. The fat stone prop stood in the way of a new tunnel excavation. They were back working where they'd done the first job, blocking off the infected *grisù* tunnel. They'd unearthed the base of the pillar and already started dismantling the column piece by piece with efficiency. Yet Ntoni worked at a sluggish pace. Thoughts of Ziu Peppi distracted him.

Malpelo stood opposite the pillar, hammering away at it with a pickaxe.

"You didn't meet us after church yesterday," he said.

"I couldn't. I wanted to see Ziu Peppi, but he's at Floristella Grottacalda now."

"Everyone is going there," Malpelo said. "All of the small mines are closing up. They're getting stricter with everything. There's too much competition. Look at these tracks they're putting in for the new carts. They're not going to let the *carusi* work anymore."

Ntoni didn't respond. Lido would soon arrive in the mines, though an exact date had not yet been given. Would it be too late to offer his mother the envelope in exchange for Lido or himself? Was it wrong if Ziu Peppi might never know? Every choice confused him. Ntoni thought of the money, which he'd kept hidden away in a large residue heap on the outskirts of the mines. Perhaps he'd be beaten or killed if the other miners discovered it on him.

He paused again to tighten the bandana around his nose and mouth. Working in this area unsettled him. All the previous demolition work made for a very unstable section, but Rosco wanted another tunnel created to reach a new vein of sulfur. Several miners stood nearby, piecing together long strips of rail track in an area of the tunnel that was already cleared. They'd been ordered to use this new space to lay new two-by-four tracks for the ore carts that would be pulled forward by mules. Rosco was anxious to step up the rate of production, keeping in line with the competition. The miners set down the portions of metal in rows much like a small railroad. Each man hunched over as he worked in a kind of beetle-like stance. The ridge of their spines were bent and marked with a series of *bottoni* — small circular scabs received from the unavoidable bumping and scraping against the tunnel's low ceiling.

They traded stories and gossip about miners who'd left for Floristella Grottacalda, and how advanced things were with better drills and machinery. Ntoni's ears perked up at the name of the rival mine, and he strained to listen, hoping to catch some news about Ziu Peppi. He made out only snippets — something about their carts being driven through the earth by a great steel cable aboveground. Perhaps Ziu Peppi operated it. Was he already training some new assistant?

Ntoni threw down his shovel and reached for a pickaxe. He moved up too fast, whacking his back against rock. The pain cut through him as if he'd been singed with a hot poker, though he tried his best to ignore it. He began to swing at the pillar, his arms alive with a vengeful rush of energy. Chips of rock scattered as he hit the edge of the pick into the column. A wide crack soon formed along the side of its base, and began deepening into a thick, arc-shaped crevice. Ntoni beat at the prop as he pushed through the suffocating heat and swallowed sulfur dust with each movement. The sliver of space he worked inside of seemed to be shrinking, as though the pit was squeezing together, compressing him into a bed of minerals. He imagined the heaviness of countless layers of earth pressing above them, separated by a few inches of open space. The ceiling groaned. Ntoni froze. His arms went limp; the pickaxe clunked to the ground.

"Did you hear that?"

"Hear what?" Malpelo continued to strike at the pillar's remains.

Ntoni pulled down the bandana and swiped at his brow. A wave of dizziness made him stop. He leaned against the wall and tried to breathe. Was he only imagining things? Ntoni studied the props that stood around them, one at each corner of the pit. The wooden planks held up the support beams and girders, bracing the natural rock that made up the ceiling. He scanned the area, checking the other miners nearby to see if they'd heard anything. They remained engrossed in talk and infrequent bursts of laughter. Everyone was always supposed to be on alert for any strange earthen groans that might herald a cave-in.

He eyed the props. Ziu Peppi once told him about the temperamental nature of the structures, given the effects of heat or construction. Some of the girders appeared to have buckled under the weight of the above world. Their warped edges forced some miners to duck under them in order to pass. He waited another moment but heard nothing. The air felt thicker than usual. Ntoni breathed again into his handkerchief but could not find relief. Tiny black specks danced before his eyes. He breathed, forcing away a sudden wave of dizziness. Then he took up his pickaxe and swung hard, desperate to steady himself, until missing the pillar completely. He tripped forward, crashing against a nearby support prop, hard enough that the walls around them shook. This, the others heard. One of the miners hollered something, and everyone dropped their tools, bracing themselves as if the ceiling might fall. The props remained intact.

After another long moment of stillness and unease, the miners confronted him, demanding to know what happened.

"Do you want to get us all killed?"

Ntoni sat against the prop, for a moment unable to breathe. He couldn't bear to raise his head. This much was sure to get back to Rosco.


Outside, Ntoni and Malpelo joined the others at the large brook near Rosco's small distillery. On such hot, suffocating afternoons as today there was little else they could do but find some relief in the cool stream. Rows of shrubbery and plane trees banked either side of the fast-moving stream. The miners became different men at the spring, laughing over stories of home. Talk of work, the subterranean life that pinned them against sulfur rock, dissolved from conversation once they immersed in the water. They scrubbed away at the yellow and brown grit caking over their skin, smoked cigarettes and passed around small woven jugs of wine brought from Raccolto or Piazza Armerina. Ntoni watched their faces for any sign that they'd been talking about him. Perhaps news of his failure had reached them all, but they continued to talk, oblivious of him.

He cupped water against his face and gargled to force the sulfur dust out from his nose and mouth. The water on his cracked lips was icy, painful but sweet as it coated the inside of his throat. He pressed wet palms against the sides of his face and relaxed. Soon he joined Malpelo and waded deeper into the brook. They splashed against one another, much to the annoyance of a few nearby miners, and laughed at the film of dirt and filth that fell from their bodies.

Ntoni pushed water through the dirt-caked strands of his hair, raking it back against his head and gazed at the other miners, some sitting nude at the edge of the stream. His eyes locked with one, whose intrusive stare gave him a visceral reaction. Ntoni looked away and tried to ignore the man, though the miner approached with a lewd smile. He was dwarf-like with a severe nose and a hard, wrinkled face. The whole of his body was covered in coarse black hairs. He reminded Ntoni of an enormous scavenging crow. He crept up beside where the *carusi* stood in the stream.

"You're Sciavelli's boy. I've heard good things about you."

72

Ntoni bobbed his head in a vague way, unwilling to engage. He frowned at Malpelo. The miner studied the wounds in Ntoni's skin, and edged closer, suggesting that if the boy got sick of working under Sciavelli then he could always come work for him. His hand grazed the side of the boy's arm, a vile tenderness in his touch. Ntoni thought of the boy he'd seen that night in the tunnels. He shuddered but said nothing, hearing again Ziu Peppi's warning. Malpelo had once told him how some boys were lured in by food and cigarettes offered in exchange for their bodies. You could not trust the miners. Ntoni clenched his teeth. How could he begin to explain any of this to Lido? He turned away for the shore, looking behind only once to see the miner still there, eyeing him.

His brother arrived later that week. Sciavelli introduced him to the other miners and *carusi* as his new assistant. Ntoni's heart stuttered. The decision was pure spite. Perhaps Sciavelli himself had convinced his mother or the Miniera Cozzo Disi to make Lido his personal assistant. Ntoni picked at the remaining trail of scabs along his face and chest. How he wished he could pull his brother away and race with him back to Raccolto. Lido appeared calm. His lips hinted at a faint smile. He would not look at Ntoni. Instead he pulled the blue bandana around his neck, fitting it over his nose and mouth as the others did. Then he disappeared with Sciavelli through the tunnels.

All throughout the day, Ntoni caught glances of Lido during breaks from his work with Malpelo or stealing away every hour or so to retrieve some unnecessary tool or double-check an instruction given by one of the miners on the job. Each time, he made sure to pass Sciavelli's pit or the staircase that the *carusi* climbed, hoping to monitor his brother's progress and well-being. Twice, Ntoni fumbled with the rock drill or almost struck his pickaxe against his shin.

"Are you OK?" Malpelo said.

"If he lays a hand on Lido just once, I'll stick this through his head." Ntoni gestured with the tool and swung. His friend laughed.

"I'll believe that when I see it."

Ntoni shook his head. He couldn't ignore Lido's struggle. He saw it in the way his brother carried his basket, overflowing with minerals. Lido walked too fast under each load, refusing to pace himself, anxious to get the job done and prove his worth. None of it would make the *soccorso morto* go away any faster. It was only a matter of time before Sciavelli's abuse or the work itself broke him.

At dusk, the day's shift over, Ntoni found Lido standing against the hut where the boys slept and gathered. His dark curls stuck against his forehead, matted together with sweat and dust; his bandana, now stained yellow and brown from sulfur fumes, hung in a limp circle around his throat. He laughed over something one of the boys said, but when he noticed Ntoni approaching, Lido's mouth tightened and he straightened his posture.

"You're not supposed to be here," Ntoni said.

Lido shared a flippant look with his new friends. "Why not?"

"Did she put you up to this?"

His brother squinted hard. "What are you talking about? *Matri* already told you what we decided when you were home. Remember?"

"She didn't tell me everything. I thought we had an agreement."

"No we didn't."

"You were supposed to wait until next month before starting here."

"Says who? I was never told that."

"Tell me someone at least explained to you what a *soccorso morto* debt means."

Lido scrunched up his face as if he might spit. "Don't you know how hard things are for us? I want to work. We need to help out. All of us."

His mother's words. Ntoni sighed. He felt deflated. There was no reasoning with his brother. The others watched with amusement, hoping for a fight. Ntoni let it drop. One of the *carusi* passed around a cigarette and the conversation shifted back to jokes and gossip. Soon Ntoni followed his brother inside to the kitchen area in the back, where a communal pot of stewed lentils sat upon a small wood-burning stove. They retrieved two small bowls from a stack on a table by the wall and waited in line with the others.

"Everyone's treating you good at least?" Ntoni said.

Lido nodded. "Sure. I love it here."

"What about the work itself?"

"Fine. My arms get tired but I'll get used to it."

"Sciavelli can get impatient."

"He said you were one of his best *carusi*."

"Did he?" Ntoni's wounds prickled.

"Yeah and that if I worked as hard then maybe I'd be even better."

"Sure. But don't let Sciavelli bully you into lifting more than what you need to right now. You shouldn't start off with such a heavy load."

His brother's face darkened. "Have you been watching me?"

"Some."

"Why? You don't think I can handle working here?"

Lido moved ahead in line, cutting past others to join his friends. Ntoni squeezed his fists but restrained himself. There was no point in starting anything foolish in front of everyone, though he failed to shake away more thoughts of Sciavelli beating and humiliating his brother.

They exchanged few words underground. Ntoni resisted the urge to monitor his brother's progress, though it surprised, even impressed him that Lido was getting on as well as he did for his first week, far better than Ntoni had when he started. Even the other *carusi* seemed to accept him without any bullying. Still, he wondered what he could do to get Lido out. Perhaps there might still be a way for Rosco to reconsider his brother's fate.

Several weeks passed. A new job brought Ntoni closer to Sciavelli's pit. He and Malpelo were ordered to assist in the construction of new rail tracks for the crates. The long hours seemed to merge together without end, distorting Ntoni's sense of time. One afternoon, as he crawled beneath the low rock ceiling of a narrow tunnel, dragging along a basket of tools, the mice began to charge at him. Dozens scurried past his hands and limbs, rushing out from the bowels of the mine. The creatures forced him to pause, unnerved. An endless pinch of tiny-clawed feet scrambled over his skin. Their frantic squeaking made him sick with knowing.

The earthen floor turned–a slow, gradual spin. The walls trembled. Black crooked mouths of nearby caves and tunnels yawned, their shadows elongating across the dim corridors. Ntoni threw down the basket. Gripping his acetone lamp, he scrambled back through the tunnels. He approached the first miner he could. The man stood, burrowing a rock drill into the wall, absorbed in his work.

"Did you feel that?" Ntoni shouted over the machine's buzz.

The miner glared, but soon felt the dizzy sway of the walls surrounding his own pit. A low rumbling emitted from the rocks. He shut off the drill and cast a long gaze over the ceiling above. Dust sprinkled out from along a crack. His eyes bulged. He grabbed his lamp and raced out, screaming.

"Cave-in! Cave-in!"

Already a thunderous roar approached, much like the growl of an ore cart in the near distance. Mice continued to race past their feet. Ntoni chilled at the touch of their furry bodies. He hurried after the miner, shouting, alerting the others, and a small crowd of workers soon joined them. They funneled into the main artery of the mine, everyone talking at once. Lamplight appeared and disappeared in sporadic bursts, a disjointed maze of shadow and panic. Frantic lines of *carusi* hurried up along the tall stairway to the glowing archway at the top of the steps. Several bodies tumbled over one another. Ntoni searched past everyone, frantic for Lido. He raced closer toward the stairway. A ferocious groan echoed through the tunnels, and the walls twitched and crumbled. Soon the roof would give.

Ntoni only caught a glimpse of the stairway's collapse. The fallen boys crushed. He screamed for Lido. A wave of dust and rubble kicked up and rushed forward. Ntoni raced back through the tunnels, colliding with others. A thick dust cloud overwhelmed the area, knocking out the acetone lamps, and submerging them all into darkness. The men screamed. They tore at one another in a sightless fury. Chords of anguish rose and fell, splintered among long hacking coughs. An explosion sounded in the distance, then another. The air was on fire, full of burning dirt and smoke. Ntoni's eyes singed. A rain of hard pellets darted against his body, followed by a large rock that struck him against the jaw. Blood soaked through his tongue.

A dim flickering emerged ahead, revealing the outline of a shaft and wide rectangular box. The elevator. Uneven shards of daylight emerged through the steel cage doors. Heat and dust shimmered in the small visible spaces above their heads. Some of the men fell against the elevator and tried to pull its doors apart, desperate to climb up the cables or find some refuge inside the empty car. Some pressed their faces against the meshing and screamed for help, hoping their cries would be lifted up through the shaft.

The rumbling stopped. One of the miners found a lamp hanging near the elevator and revealed a wall of rocks that blocked the passage from where they'd come, though another tunnel remained open nearby. Ntoni knew that this one emptied out into Sciavelli's pit, and he remembered the ladder that led aboveground through the ventilation shaft. He pushed past the others who told him to stay put. It might take hours, if not days for someone to dig them out. There was no telling when or if another cave-in would erupt. Ntoni pushed past them and squeezed back through the tunnels, shoving himself forward in the darkness. Others trailed close behind, doubtful of rescue.

He rounded another corner where a pair of eyes shot out from the weak lamplight. Ntoni jumped back. Sciavelli's face emerged from the shadows, covered in soot and blood.

"What are you still doing here?"

"Where's Lido?"

The miner struggled for breath as he limped forward. "He already took his basket to the furnaces."

Ntoni turned but Sciavelli caught him by the arm.

"Don't you smell the fire? These tunnels could explode at any moment. Get back to the elevator!"

"I need to find Lido!"

"He's not here. He must've made it out. Go back!"

"It's not running. The only way out is through the ventilator shaft."

Sciavelli's gaze trained on him for a moment before he handed over the lamp. He followed Ntoni at a hobbled gait. Blood covered his thighs. Soon they reached the wide mouth of the ventilation shaft, its rope ladder still intact. Other miners joined them.

"That's a two-hundred-foot climb," Sciavelli said.

Ntoni gripped its rungs and pulled himself up into the chute. The rope felt too thin and flimsy. Another tremor shook the walls. Rocks fell back around them, but they pulled themselves through the shaft—a compressed space, maybe two feet wide, barely enough for the men to fit themselves through. They squeezed themselves up. Ntoni climbed, forcing himself up along each desperate inch of braided leather and twine that wore on and chafed against his raw palms. If he slipped, his fall would topple those beneath him. Perhaps the rope would give out, snapping under their weight. The climb felt endless. Ntoni's muscles burned. His movement slowed. The dizziness returned. His grip loosened with each rung. Then the rope tugged with such violence that Ntoni shrieked and wrapped himself around the thin ladder as he waited for the rope to snap.

"The rope's too heavy! It's breaking!"

Ntoni cut his eyes to Sciavelli, whose legs worked in savage thrusts, kicking at the hands and faces of those behind him, forcing the men to drop, their screams echoing down the long metal tunnel. Then he turned and reached forward. Ntoni scrambled up the ladder and pulled himself out of the shaft.

A crowd of surviving miners and *carusi* stood around at the surface, helping pull bodies from the rubble and ventilation shafts. Some ventured back into the smoldering darkness to deliver others to safety. The men they pulled out had burnt, disfigured limbs and mouths blackened with soot. Ntoni moved past them, screaming for his brother. He made for the *discenderia*. If there was any chance of finding Lido buried alive, he'd be there. The wide arched door leading to the *carusi*'s stairway had collapsed, leaving behind a mound of thick stone fragments and smoking debris. Ntoni went to his knees, clawing his way past the endless pile of dirt and rocks, though he dreaded the sudden discovery of a bloodied limb or his brother's face. Burning dust clouded the air, stinging his eyes and skin. He dug, his hands furious and raw. His throat ached as he sobbed for Lido.

"Get away from there! It's not stable!"

A man gripped his shoulder and yanked him upright. Ntoni scratched and tore at his arms and hands. Another miner appeared. The men hauled him away without much effort, tossing his body clear. Ntoni rose, dazed but no longer weeping.

"My brother," he said.

One of the men cocked his head with sudden interest.

"There's a rescue crew coming from Piazza Armerina. Stand aside and wait until they arrive," he said.

Ntoni opened his mouth to further explain but then Sciavelli appeared in the distance. He thought of him inside the shaft, kicking the other miners down, falling to their deaths, and his stomach became weak. Ntoni raced through the confused

81

throng, past the basins and the furnaces to where the gray heaps of sulfur dirt stood. He glanced behind to make sure that Sciavelli wasn't trailing him, but saw only an unending tail of black smoke leaving the mine site, tracing the sky in thick veins of shadow.

Ntoni sat inside of the *cimitero* for a long time, waiting in an old rusted barrel that once held sulfur bricks. He gripped Ziu Peppi's envelope to his chest, having unearthed it before hiding, and wept. For a moment, he feared that his cries might somehow be heard by Sciavelli or another miner, but found that he was unable to stop. There was nothing to do now but to wait for the rescue crew. Voices of men, muffled but frantic, echoed across the mounds of dirt surrounding the deserted scrap yard. Ntoni's fingernails bled. A yellow crust of dirt coated over his hands. Gashes oozed along the length of his arms. His mouth continued to bleed. He inspected the cut gums with a careful finger, discovered a missing tooth and winced. Debris had fallen against him during the escape. How long would it take for the rescuers to arrive? Perhaps they were already here. Lido's face shadowed each thought. Ntoni considered going back but found his bones stiff and unmovable, weighted by fatigue. He shut his eyes and tried to sleep. An image of Sciavelli floated through his half-conscious state. The miner stood before a large hole in the earth, stamping his feet. A smoldering fire rose from deep inside of the pit. The tips of a ladder stood up through the opening. Ntoni squinted against the burning smoke. Hands reached from the mouth of the shaft—other *carusi*, trying to pull themselves out of the inferno. Sciavelli kicked at them until they were swallowed into the black throat of the mine. Then he knocked the ladder over. Ntoni stood, unable to move or look away. Ash continued to sting his eyes. He watched the hole and waited for the hands to reemerge. He'd pull them out somehow, even if Sciavelli was there, ready to stomp on them. Ntoni waited. The hands would not come.

He woke, breathless. His fingers moved up along the inside of the barrel, for a moment uncertain of whether he was still underground. Then he crawled out into the scrap yard. Discarded bits of tools and machine parts surrounded him, lit by a sun half-obscured by smoke. The air tasted burnt and he choked hard, spitting up blood. His jawbone ached. He resisted the urge to probe the empty socket with his tongue. The *cimitero* remained deserted. Perhaps an hour or so had passed. He pressed a hand against his brow. The daylight made him nauseous. One of his eyes was bruised into a raised slit. Ntoni checked again that all of his fingers and limbs had made it out unbroken. He felt for the envelope, still there, tied beneath the folds of his loincloth. Ntoni imagined Lido, bloodied and dazed among the survivors. He hurried back to the others.

They stacked the dead in piles at the back of several mule-driven carts, a long white sheet secured over the bodies. Several wounded men sat together, while others tended to their wounds, and pieced together makeshift splints to support broken limbs. Ntoni moved past in long, anxious strides, his gaze relentless. Smoke still clouded the air, undercutting the dank smell of sulfur. Small groups of men stood near the collapsed mine shaft with shovels, digging through the rubble. Ahead stood a long row of survivors who waited to be processed before their release. Ntoni overheard that Rosco had arranged for their transportation back home.

Moans rose from everywhere around.

At the entrance point building, an unending line of miners and *carusi* gathered. Each survivor bent his head as he leaned closer to where the clerk told him to sign. Everyone needed to be accounted for. Ntoni pushed through, checking the book for Lido's name, but stopped when prodded to sign his own—to do so would only bind him to the mines forever. The *soccorso morto* could only be forgiven in death. Malpelo's red hair caught his attention. His friend stood near the front of the line. When Malpelo looked up, Ntoni snapped his head down before his friend could catch sight of him. It was better this way. He could not sign his name in the survivors' book. Ntoni hurried through the dazed throng, and returned to the *cimitero*. He could not be seen by others. He crawled inside of the barrel and waited until evening drove the men away.

The Miniera Cozzo Disi emitted an absolute stillness that night. His footsteps crunched over gravel, echoing along the darkened path. No burning lamplights glowed in the windows, not even from Rosco's palace. Gray strips of moonlight shone against the silent furnace domes and elevator towers. It was as if the entire mining site stood holding its breath, waiting for some further destruction to unfold. Ntoni hurried onward. He felt watched. Long wooden planks boarded up the mouth of the *discenderia*. It was uncertain whether the miners had succeeded in digging out the *carusi* or if any of the boys had escaped at all. Perhaps Lido was already home. Ntoni imagined his brother trembling, trying to communicate to their mother what happened in breathless, tearful gasps, unable to keep up the tough facade any longer. His brother alive but shaken. Ntoni clung to this thought as he made his way forward.

He squeezed past the entrance gate with ease but found it difficult to follow the curve of the road from where it bent through the dense black meadows. His raw, bruised feet pinched against dirt and stones. But soon the fields outside of the Miniera Cozzo Disi comforted him. Clusters of starlight fit against the sky, returning a soft glow to the night. The steady chirp and hum of mosquitoes and crickets resumed its place at his ear, and he smiled. Fireflies punctured the darkness, the brief warm flicker of their glow illuminating the unseen passages that surrounded him. When Ntoni reached Raccolto's lights, his legs stiffened. In a few weeks, perhaps less, the Miniera Cozzo Disi would reopen, the damage cleared out. Everyone back to work. And yet he never signed his name in the survivors' book. He felt again for the envelope, tucked away in the folds of his loincloth. Perhaps somehow it wasn't too late to buy back his and Lido's freedom if his brother survived. Ntoni's eyes stung. Fatigue spread through his limbs, forcing him to sit for a moment in the tall, dry grass, where the weeds reached above his shoulders. He hugged his legs into his chest and wept.

*Matri* seldom locked the front door. Ntoni opened it just enough to fit his body inside, careful not to make any sound. The house was very still as he crept through, his feet damp against the cool tile floor. Thin slivers of weak gray light slipped in through the curtained windows, outlining the meager bits of furniture, the iron tub and tall ladder leading upstairs to the loft. Perhaps his mother was already awake, waiting for him. The house appeared to be deserted. He entered the small kitchen where his church suit hung among a pile of laundry on one of the countertops, still wet from a recent washing. Twilight soaked through the small window overlooking the garden. His mother sat hunched over in a chair beneath one of the almond trees.

He crept outside. An early morning breeze tickled through his hair, bringing with it a smell of eucalyptus that caught in his throat. Twilight edged along the neighboring rooftops and tree branches. An arc of pink and gold grew along the horizon, highlighting his mother's pinched features, the way her black lace shawl draped over her head and gathered around the shoulders of her thin housedress. He stood before her and whispered.

"*Matri.*"

She jerked awake. Her eyes widened at the sight of him as she sat up, rigid and straight, her gaze bright and intense. Then she rose, her movements slow and careful, before she knelt beside him. She grasped at his arms and hands, pressing her fingertips against his skin, as if to make sure he was real.

"Is Lido upstairs?" he said.

She bent her head, unable to respond, and released her hold on him. His mother sank into a heap against the grass. The whole of her trembled as she wept.

Ntoni fled back into the house and climbed up the bedroom ladder. Lido wasn't there. He tore apart the straw mattress that he and his brother once shared and beat his palms against its thin wire frame. From a corner opposite the room, his sister Lina watched him, her eyes large and wet.

His mother forbade him to leave the house for weeks. Nor was he allowed to go near any of the windows, which she kept shut under heavy curtains. Ntoni became delirious. He raced through the tunnels in his sleep, reaching for his brother before Lido was swallowed beneath the falling ceiling. Lina sat beside him when he awoke, screaming. She pressed a damp cloth against his feverish skin and listened while he tried to describe what happened through incoherent fragments. Unending images swirled in his mind of Lido suffocating inside one of the ventilator shafts, or left alive for days, only to endure a slow death, his body trapped beneath the crushed stairway. His brother's cries echoed through the tunnels unheard.

87

He held nothing back from Lina, unable to spare her the more gruesome details of the cave-in, though it failed to dampen her curiosity. She shadowed Ntoni through the rooms, probing him again with questions about the mines and working with Lido.

"I've told you everything already. I can't go over it anymore," he said.

"What about this?"

She handed him a large envelope stamped with the Miniera Cozzo Disi's official red emblem. Ntoni withdrew a single photograph about the size of his hand. He traced a fingertip over the smooth glossy texture of the print, where a smiling image of himself and Malpelo stood in their loincloths outside of the *discenderia*'s wide stone mouth. Against the overexposed black and white, Ntoni's scar was difficult to make out. A hard light shown in his eyes and teeth, distorting his features with brightness.

"*Matri* was keeping it in her bureau. Who's that you're with?" Lina said.

Ntoni fit the picture back into its envelope. "It doesn't matter," he said, his voice low and empty.

*Matri* refused to open the door when neighbors came to share their condolences. Even the priest wasn't allowed inside. She let Raccolto believe that both of her sons were lost. The *Chiesa Madre* held a special memorial service for the fallen *carusi* — so many had gone missing that all of Raccolto was forced together in mourning over it. This his mother attended with Lina. Ntoni remained alone at home. He didn't try to fight her decision to hide him though he knew that the Miniera Cozzo Disi would soon find out about his survival. There was no escaping it. She shared what the community knew about the cave-in. The details haunted him—another pillar had collapsed in one of the areas where he and Malpelo had excavated, and its fall brought down a portion of the roof. Perhaps they blamed him for it. One evening at the kitchen table, he shared with her every terrible detail of the cave-in, Sciavelli's violence, his failure to rescue Lido, the shame Ntoni felt in not signing the survivors' book. Then he gave her Ziu Peppi's envelope. She could do with it what she would.

"This is *Patri*'s money too," he said.

"His earnings?"

Ntoni shook his head. "Didn't he ever tell you about his plans to leave Sicily? He wanted to go to France and be a miner there. Ziu Peppi told me there was more money in it. He was arranging the paperwork for *Patri* so he could travel and work. He helped a lot of miners out that way."

His mother's gaze widened. "Your father would never leave us like that."

"He never told you anything?"

"Never."

"Maybe he didn't know how to tell you."

She sighed, her eyes becoming wet. "He could be so quiet about things sometimes. So secretive."

"Maybe he wanted more for us. Ziu Peppi tried to help him. He was trying to help me too."

His mother frowned. "Who's to say your friend wasn't planning on just keeping the money for himself? Do you really think he cared that much about you or us for that matter? How many others did you know personally who were actually helped by him?"

"He always told me not to talk about it with anyone." Ntoni paused and shook his head. Fresh pain expanded from the spot where Ziu Peppi's silence wounded him. "I guess it doesn't really matter now. The money is yours," he said.

"Why do you keep saying that? You never signed your name in that book. Are you sure no one saw you leave?"

"Yes," Ntoni lied. Thoughts of Sciavelli chilled him.

*Matri* rested a hand against her brow. "I will never get it out of my head, that moment I heard the sirens, the women crying in the streets. Then I knew. I knew before I saw the carts full of men coming back from the mines. The bodies wrapped in sheets. Just like when your father died. I knew."

Later in the week, the mine reopened for business. Ntoni's mother spent most of her time alone in the garden, shelling almonds. Her long dark hair hung around her shoulders, messy and unwashed. One morning she rose early to pack a small suitcase and announced that she and Lina would take a short trip to Catania to visit some relatives who might be able to help.

Any hope they had now rested in her long-forgotten clan, aided by the influence of Ziu Peppi's money.

They returned home after a few days. Ntoni's mother took him aside in the kitchen and told him how it was all arranged — he'd be shipped to an American port that neither of them could pronounce, where he'd assist some cousin on the dockyards, sending back what earnings he could. He'd be with family there. Perhaps it'd be a new start for all of them.

She handed him enough money to keep himself fed, along with a thin satchel of clothing, and an address in Catania. The city buses seldom reached this far into the country, unless he opted for the train, but then he'd be seen for sure. Only the sulfur trucks from the Miniera Cozzo Disi left for Catania. They'd be the best means of transportation if Ntoni was willing to take the risk. He trembled hard. His mother grazed her knuckles against his face and smiled.

Later that night, he slipped through their door and out onto the deserted streets.

A diesel engine woke him. Ntoni had slept behind the mine's vacant sentry box, where shipments were processed and received early the next morning. Now he crouched in the tall grass. The lone attendant stood with two truckers, who'd come for the latest batch of sulfur barrels. They faced the direction of the furnaces, sharing what little they knew about the cave-in. One of the men wore a knit cap and suspenders that Ntoni recognized. He strained his neck a bit, as if he could make out the mineshafts from afar. Ntoni struggled to listen above the motor's hum. Only fragmented bits of their conversation reached him, though Rosco's name continued to pass between them with scorn.

The truck's rear cargo area looked to be already loaded. Ntoni sensed that the men would soon depart. He moved fast. The open bed at the back of the truck was not as packed with barrels as on other days, so Ntoni found it easier to squeeze into a corner between the drums of sulfur once he climbed aboard. He stretched himself as flat as the tight space would allow and prayed that he couldn't be seen in the rearview mirror. The truck swayed a bit when the men returned to their seats. Ntoni held his breath as the engine revved and the truck lurched forward, causing some of the barrels to tremble. A rush of electricity coursed through him. His body absorbed every bump and mechanical snarl along the way.

He remained still throughout most of the ride, afraid that the slightest movement might expose him. Perhaps the truckers would beat him if they knew that he'd smuggled aboard, then take his money and leave him deserted on the side of the road. How far had they traveled from Raccolto? Muffled voices, the occasional bark of laughter, escaped through the open windows, and were chewed up by the rambling motor. Ntoni dozed, only to be jerked awake by a jolt in the road. Cold, salted air rushed across his face. He propped himself up on his elbows, just enough to peek over the side of the truck. Catania emerged, whipping ahead — the tops and edges of gray ornate buildings appeared carved into one another in long expansive rows. The city awed him, and beyond it appeared the steel-tipped waves of the Mediterranean Sea. For a moment, Ntoni forgot himself and sat up for a better look. Then he snapped his head in the direction of the truckers, where he met one's stare in the rearview mirror.

Ntoni shot back down. He curled up into his corner behind the barrels. He was done for now. They'd drag him out and take turns beating him. The noise and movement of the truck became heightened to his senses. Instead they kept driving. Ntoni's lungs burned until the vehicle slowed and came to a gradual stop. Harbor noises — boat horns, a jangle of chains and strange machinery, men shouting orders — hung in his ears. He squeezed his body tighter. The doors slammed open and shut. Footsteps crunched outside around the truck. Their voices became soft and indistinguishable above the roar in Ntoni's head. The back safety door unlatched. His jaw tensed. Each barrel slid out, its rusted end scraping along the open bed of the truck. When the last drum was pulled forward, Ntoni felt a hot presence upon him. He peeled himself out from the corner, turning his head to meet the gaze of the man he'd seen in the rearview mirror. The mover wore a knit cap and suspenders. His stare was bright and curious. Then after a long moment, he latched the door shut and turned away.

"We're all set here," he said to the others.

Ntoni froze, uncertain. Only when the engine fired up did he scramble off the truck and stumble onto the hard gravel below.

He hurried through the dockyard. Various cargo ships and small fishing trawlers stood anchored along the wharf. He hitched the satchel over his shoulder, feeling again for the address buried deep in his pocket. He couldn't bring himself to look back, half-expecting a wild chorus of shouts, the men clamoring after him. But instead the dock workers remained absorbed in their business, moving wooden crates between the nearby warehouses and long planks for the vessels that awaited them.

Catania overwhelmed him. The streets were wide and long, full of people and trams that ran on endless strips of electrical wire and steel tracks, stopping at intervals throughout the city. Tall Baroque buildings made of marble and gray lava stone lined the sidewalks. Long ropey tendrils of spider plants hung between the intricate black iron balustrades of balconies. Grinning masks and delicate cherubs stood out among the decorative flourishes and curves of some buildings. Others were no more than towering heaps of rubble — remnants of the war.

He had to ask for directions several times. The address led him to a section of town where the houses stood in ruin. Their gray stucco walls appeared thin and weathered, while other houses appeared to be abandoned. Deserted rooms shone through glassless windows, cluttered with wooden planks and random debris strewn together inside. Those Ntoni passed, soon finding the house in question, a small dismal place with a sagging tile rooftop. He knocked hard. All of Catania's heat and motor exhaust seemed embedded in his clothes and skin.

An older woman appeared at the door. She wore her gray hair in a stylish cut just past her chin. Her dark eyes flickered with scrutiny beneath her thick glasses.

"I'm Regina Giordano's son," Ntoni said.

The woman's brow smoothed and a smile softened her wrinkled mouth.

"So, the dead walk among us?" she said.

Ntoni squinted, uncertain how to respond. The woman laughed.

"*Scordatilu*. Relax. Your mother showed me that photograph of you and some other boy in the mines. Come inside."

A scent of dried jasmine and bitter orange peels greeted Ntoni as he followed her into the house. She led him to a room with small, delicate furniture and a tall record player that stood among large potted floor plants. The walls were bare except for a framed painting of the Madonna, her eyes raised in devotion. He sat beside the woman on a firm sofa, nervous that he'd dirty its crème-colored fabric with his person.

"In another life, you might have called me *zia*," the woman said. "But Antonella or Ana is fine. We all make our own choices, don't we? Your mother chose to stay in Raccolto. She loved your father. She martyred herself for him. And now your brother. How much can she endure?"

"I don't know," Ntoni said. Thoughts of his father and brother hollowed him out. The woman rose, and he followed her to a small room behind the kitchen, furnished with a narrow cot and lone bureau. He'd stay here for a few weeks until his documents were ready. She spoke with warmth of those who'd greet him in America, but Ntoni only half-listened, her words strange and thin.

She woke him that next morning with warm milk and a fresh *cornetto* filled with marmalade. Ntoni sat in a corner of Antonella's kitchen, studying his mother's sister in quiet awe, uncertain of what to say. He'd received a house key and a small wrinkled map of Catania from her, along with a stern request to lock the door before leaving. Most afternoons she spent managing a small fishing equipment store that her husband owned. Ntoni never met his uncle, though he heard the old man shuffling through the rooms at night and in the early morning. Perhaps it seemed unnecessary given their estrangement or Ntoni's approaching departure. Still, Antonella treated him with curious affection, even buying him new clothing and shoes. Often, she brought up his mother.

"It took her years to visit me. Such a shame really, but I am used to waiting. It's the one thing I've truly known. Did your mother ever tell you how we'd wait for our father and brothers when they went out to sea with the other fishermen? They'd be gone for weeks at a time. Some fishermen never returned. There was nothing you could do about it. Then one morning, a bell would ring in the *piazza* and the other mothers and children would come out to greet the men in the harbor. We'd watch them unload all of the fish they caught. I still remember how it felt to touch my father's sleeves and smell him."

Ntoni thought of *Patri* coming home from the mines, his brow knit with exhaustion, the lines around his eyes and mouth carrying traces of sulfur dust. The whole week seemed to build up to that moment each Sunday morning when his father returned home again. How the family gathered around him in wonder and relief.

Antonella placed a hand on his shoulder and smiled. "Don't look so sad. Any day now we'll have you ready to go," she said.

He had no choice but to trust her.

She took him to the Feast of Saint Agatha later that next week, not long after showing him his ticket for the *SS Dabbanna*, along with the necessary paperwork. Saint Agatha was the city's patron saint, making the day one of the region's biggest holidays. Later, there might even be fireworks, his aunt claimed. Catania's population seemed to double overnight—every cobblestone street and alleyway became overwhelmed with people. It was early evening. The sticky mid-August heat continued to thicken the air. They moved along Via Garibaldi, closer to the procession. Antonella maneuvered her petite frame through the crowds and past carts selling *granita de limone*, fried *panelle*, *gelato* and marzipan fruit. She strained her thin neck for a better look past the others who pressed in close against them. Ntoni tensed over the lack of space, feeling again the low ceilings and narrow tunnels of the mines.

A group of men hoisted Saint Agatha's bronze, gem and pearl-studded statue upon their shoulders and delivered her forward. She clasped a palm branch in one hand and the Bible in the other. Light soaked through her crown, winking against the sun. A small brass band played, its heavy drumbeat herding the crowd onward. Hordes of people pushed against one another, and soon Ntoni and Antonella were swept along with them. For a moment, the statue trembled sideways, and he cringed at the thought of it falling over. Instead, the men bearing the saint paused in their march and allowed the crowd to come closer. Men and women rush forward, eager to touch Saint Agatha's feet with their hands and lips. They knocked against Ntoni's shoulders and limbs, pushing him aside in a frenzy of devotion. Men lifted squealing babies and toddlers high up in the air, passing them from one man to another, until the crying faces reached the lips and cheeks of the saint. Soon young children and older people joined them.

"Ntoni! Come here," Antonella said.

She moved toward the men, a look of joy brightening her features, as their hands reached around her, pulling her up between them. Some grabbed around her rear while others grasped her arms and legs. The hands were all around her, pushing her up, up, up into the face of the saint. Bodies shoved past Ntoni, and for a moment, he feared he might be trampled beneath them. Memories of the cave-in rushed through his mind. Once more he heard the thunderous crash of collapsing walls and the cries of fallen men — Lido screaming for help. Someone tugged at Ntoni's shoulder and tried to pull him forward, but instead he clawed at the hand and tore away.

He raced through the streets where the procession crowds thinned, not stopping until he reached the harbor's edge, to the end of a deserted pier. A wet breeze cooled his face as he studied the stucco buildings across the bay. Mount Etna loomed above, exhaling fat tendrils of smoke that fed into the clouds. Jagged strips of snow and ice veined along its towering neck. Fishing trawlers and cargo vessels stood anchored in calm waters. Ntoni sat for a while, as if he might see his own ship soon approaching. Pink and orange light danced along the tips of the Mediterranean. The ocean looked just as he hoped it would.

It is estimated that thousands of people over several generations became victims of the soccorso morto system. Although the Italian government passed legislation in 1886 restricting children under the age of nine from working in mines, quarries, and factories, these labor laws were not strictly enforced, especially in more rural and impoverished areas of Sicily, allowing abusive conditions to continue for decades more.

The Hunger Saint is the result of years of research and a collection of oral histories from the surviving miners of the Valguarnera Caropepe region in Sicily.

## ACKNOWLEDGMENTS

My parents, Peter and Joan Cerrone, have made so much
possible for me in so many ways. I thank them for their many
years of encouragement and support. My sister, Ashley Cerrone,
has been an invaluable presence in providing translation help,
cultural insight and feedback on different drafts of this book.
I first learned about the *carusi* through a Sicilian language
class organized by Domenic Giampino of the Sicilian Cultural
Institute of America in New York City. This class set me on a
long journey to Sicily and back again. I am grateful for the help
and guidance of Dr. Salvatore Di Vita of La Miniera Floristella
Grottacalda, who introduced me to many of the surviving
miners of Valguarnera Caropepe, along with Mario La Mattina
and Francesco Lo Monaco, the founders of Il Museo Lega
Zolfatai in Piazza Armerina. Dr. Chiara Mazzucchelli was
instrumental in connecting me to many generous people of the
region, especially Dorianna La Delfa, Joe La Delfa, Giovanni
Gulino and the Mazzucchelli family, who offered invaluable
insight and help. Most importantly, I especially want to thank
those former sulfur miners who were so generous in sharing
their experiences with me: Filippo Ilardi, Pietro Monaco, Andrea
Alberti, Alfredo Leuzzo and Fillippo Alberghina.

I want to extend my deepest thanks to Anthony Tamburri, Fred Gardaphe and Paolo Giordano, who were essential in getting this book into the world. Big thanks to Nick Grosso for his generous editorial guidance and patience. I also want to thank Lisa Cicchetti and Sara Zwicker for their talent and support on the graphic design of the book. Special thanks to the Museo d'Arte Moderna "Mario Rimoldi" for granting permission to use Renato Guttuso's "La Zolfara." I want to thank Henry Ferrini and everyone at the Gloucester Writers Center for supporting me with a writing residency. Much of the initial draft of the novella was completed during that time. I am also indebted to the support of writing fellowships from the Sewanee Writers' Conference, the Tin House Summer Writer's Workshop, the Ragdale Foundation, the Virginia Center for the Creative Arts, the Vermont Studio Center, Starry Night Retreat, Kimmel Harding Nelson Center for the Arts, The Noepe Center Residency, Art Farm and the Hambidge Center for the Creative Arts and Sciences. I am grateful to the SDSU Writers' Conference, who awarded an earlier version of *The Hunger Saint* with a 2014 "Conference Choice Award." I want to thank Rachel Mangini who published an excerpt of *The Hunger Saint* in *Hot Metal Bridge*. Thanks to Pap Khouma of *El-Ghibli* and the editors of *ScrittInediti* who published excerpts of the book in Italian. Thank you to Laura Romano for her beautiful translation work. A big thank you to Giovanni Morreale and *The Times of Sicily* for your support.

I want to thank the brilliant manuscript readers whose keen insight pushed me to make the book better: Greta Schuler, Kimberly Ann Southwick, Sativa January, Blair Hurley, Scott Greenan, and Catherine Parnell. Thanks to the friends and colleagues who have offered invaluable moral support and encouragement over the years, especially Shamar Hill, Courtney

McDermott, Jordan Mckenzie, Lina L. Faller, Rachel Ellick, Diana Lynch, Laurette Viteritti-Folk, Michelle Messina Reale, Rick Reiken, Rusty Barnes, Lindsay Hatton McClelland, Tony Casey of the Cultural Legacy of European Mining, Elise Capron, Laren McClung, John Domini, Tony Ardizzone, Alison Barker, Jenny Johnson, Elizabeth Kadetsky, Amy Bergen, Nicki Gill, Mark P. Lawley, Lisa Locascio, Amy Bonnaffons, Laura Rena Murray, Laurie Ducharme Lepik, Mark Spano, Karen La Rosa, Nina Ha, Rita Watson, Christina Askounis, Thaïs Miller, Maria Lisella, Anthony V. Riccio, Salvatore Scibona, Edi Giunta, Domenica Ruta, Maria Terrone, and Jennifer Martelli.

My biggest thanks goes out to Alan Zwicker, whose love inspired me to pull this manuscript out of the drawer and try again. Thank you.

## *VIA* FOLIOS
*A refereed book series dedicated to the culture of Italians and Italian Americans.*

GARIBLADI M. LAPOLLA. *Miss Rollins in Love.* Vol 119. Novel. $24
JOSEPH TUSIANI. *A Clarion Call.* Vol 118. Poetry. $16
JOSEPH A. AMATO. *My Three Sicilies.* Vol 117. Poetry & Prose. $17
MARGHERITA COSTA. *Voice of a Virtuosa and Coutesan.* Vol 116. Poetry. $24
NICOLE SANTALUCIA. *Because I Did Not Die.* Vol 115. Poetry. $12
MARK CIABATTARI. *Preludes to History.* Vol 114. Poetry. $12
HELEN BAROLINI. *Visits.* Vol 113. Novel. $22
ERNESTO LIVORNI. *The Fathers' America.* Vol 112. Poetry. $14
MARIO B. MIGNONE. *The Story of My People.* Vol 111. Non-fiction. $17
GEORGE GUIDA. *The Sleeping Gulf.* Vol 110. Poetry. $14
JOEY NICOLETTI. *Reverse Graffiti.* Vol 109. Poetry. $14
GIOSE RIMANELLI. *Il mestiere del furbo.* Vol 108. Criticism. $20
LEWIS TURCO. *The Hero Enkido.* Vol 107. Poetry. $14
AL TACCONELLI. *Perhaps Fly.* Vol 106. Poetry. $14
RACHEL GUIDO DEVRIES. *A Woman Unknown in Her Bones.* Vol 105. Poetry. $11
BERNARD BRUNO. *A Tear and a Tear in My Heart.* Vol 104. Non-fiction. $20
FELIX STEFANILE. *Songs of the Sparrow.* Vol 103. Poetry. $30
FRANK POLIZZI. *A New Life with Bianca.* Vol 102. Poetry. $10
GIL FAGIANI. *Stone Walls.* Vol 101. Poetry. $14
LOUISE DESALVO. *Casting Off.* Vol 100. Fiction. $22
MARY JO BONA. *I Stop Waiting for You.* Vol 99. Poetry. $12
RACHEL GUIDO DEVRIES. *Stati zitt, Josie.* Vol 98. Children's Literature. $8
GRACE CAVALIERI. *The Mandate of Heaven.* Vol 97. Poetry. $14
MARISA FRASCA. *Via incanto.* Vol 96. Poetry. $12
DOUGLAS GLADSTONE. *Carving a Niche for Himself.* Vol 95. History. $12
MARIA TERRONE. *Eye to Eye.* Vol 94. Poetry. $14
CONSTANCE SANCETTA. *Here in Cerchio.* Vol 93. Local History. $15
MARIA MAZZIOTTI GILLAN. *Ancestors' Song.* Vol 92. Poetry. $14
MICHAEL PARENTI. *Waiting for Yesterday: Pages from a Street Kid's Life.* Vol 90.
    Memoir. $15
ANNIE LANZILOTTO. *Schistsong.* Vol 89. Poetry. $15
EMANUEL DI PASQUALE. *Love Lines.* Vol 88. Poetry. $10
CAROSONE & LOGIUDICE. *Our Naked Lives.* Vol 87. Essays. $15
JAMES PERICONI. *Strangers in a Strange Land: A Survey of Italian-Language
    American Books.*Vol 86. Book History. $24
DANIELA GIOSEFFI. *Escaping La Vita Della Cucina.* Vol 85. Essays. $22
MARIA FAMÀ. *Mystics in the Family.* Vol 84. Poetry. $10
ROSSANA DEL ZIO. *From Bread and Tomatoes to Zuppa di Pesce "Ciambotto".*
    Vol. 83. $15
LORENZO DELBOCA. *Polentoni.* Vol 82. Italian Studies. $15
SAMUEL GHELLI. *A Reference Grammar.* Vol 81. Italian Language. $36

ROSS TALARICO. *Sled Run*. Vol 80. Fiction. $15
FRED MISURELLA. *Only Sons*. Vol 79. Fiction. $14
FRANK LENTRICCHIA. *The Portable Lentricchia*. Vol 78. Fiction. $16
RICHARD VETERE. *The Other Colors in a Snow Storm*. Vol 77. Poetry. $10
GARIBALDI LAPOLLA. *Fire in the Flesh*. Vol 76 Fiction & Criticism. $25
GEORGE GUIDA. *The Pope Stories*. Vol 75 Prose. $15
ROBERT VISCUSI. *Ellis Island*. Vol 74. Poetry. $28
ELENA GIANINI BELOTTI. *The Bitter Taste of Strangers Bread*. Vol 73. Fiction. $24
PINO APRILE. *Terroni*. Vol 72. Italian Studies. $20
EMANUEL DI PASQUALE. *Harvest*. Vol 71. Poetry. $10
ROBERT ZWEIG. *Return to Naples*. Vol 70. Memoir. $16
AIROS & CAPPELLI. *Guido*. Vol 69. Italian/American Studies. $12
FRED GARDAPHÉ. *Moustache Pete is Dead! Long Live Moustache Pete!*. Vol 67.
    Literature/Oral History. $12
PAOLO RUFFILLI. *Dark Room/Camera oscura*. Vol 66. Poetry. $11
HELEN BAROLINI. *Crossing the Alps*. Vol 65. Fiction. $14
COSMO FERRARA. *Profiles of Italian Americans*. Vol 64. Italian Americana. $16
GIL FAGIANI. *Chianti in Connecticut*. Vol 63. Poetry. $10
BASSETTI & D'ACQUINO. *Italic Lessons*. Vol 62. Italian/American Studies. $10
CAVALIERI & PASCARELLI, Eds. *The Poet's Cookbook*. Vol 61. Poetry/Recipes. $12
EMANUEL DI PASQUALE. *Siciliana*. Vol 60. Poetry. $8
NATALIA COSTA, Ed. *Bufalini*. Vol 59. Poetry. $18.
RICHARD VETERE. *Baroque*. Vol 58. Fiction. $18.
LEWIS TURCO. *La Famiglia/The Family*. Vol 57. Memoir. $15
NICK JAMES MILETI. *The Unscrupulous*. Vol 56. Humanities. $20
BASSETTI. ACCOLLA. D'AQUINO. *Italici: An Encounter with Piero Bassetti*.
    Vol 55. Italian Studies. $8
GIOSE RIMANELLI. *The Three-legged One*. Vol 54. Fiction. $15
CHARLES KLOPP. *Bele Antiche Stòrie*. Vol 53. Criticism. $25
JOSEPH RICAPITO. *Second Wave*. Vol 52. Poetry. $12
GARY MORMINO. *Italians in Florida*. Vol 51. History. $15
GIANFRANCO ANGELUCCI. *Federico F*. Vol 50. Fiction. $15
ANTHONY VALERIO. *The Little Sailor*. Vol 49. Memoir. $9
ROSS TALARICO. *The Reptilian Interludes*. Vol 48. Poetry. $15
RACHEL GUIDO DE VRIES. *Teeny Tiny Tino's Fishing Story*. Vol 47.
    Children's Literature. $6
EMANUEL DI PASQUALE. *Writing Anew*. Vol 46. Poetry. $15
MARIA FAMÀ. *Looking For Cover*. Vol 45. Poetry. $12
ANTHONY VALERIO. *Toni Cade Bambara's One Sicilian Night*. Vol 44. Poetry. $10
EMANUEL CARNEVALI. *Furnished Rooms*. Vol 43. Poetry. $14
BRENT ADKINS. et al., Ed. *Shifting Borders. Negotiating Places*. Vol 42. Conference. $18
GEORGE GUIDA. *Low Italian*. Vol 41. Poetry. $11
GARDAPHÈ, GIORDANO, TAMBURRI. *Introducing Italian Americana*. Vol 40.
    Italian/American Studies. $10
DANIELA GIOSEFFI. *Blood Autumn/Autunno di sangue*. Vol 39. Poetry. $15/$25
FRED MISURELLA. *Lies to Live By*. Vol 38. Stories. $15
STEVEN BELLUSCIO. *Constructing a Bibliography*. Vol 37. Italian Americana. $15

ANTHONY JULIAN TAMBURRI, Ed. *Italian Cultural Studies 2002*. Vol 36.
Essays. $18

BEA TUSIANI. *con amore*. Vol 35. Memoir. $19

FLAVIA BRIZIO-SKOV, Ed. *Reconstructing Societies in the Aftermath of War*.
Vol 34. History. $30

TAMBURRI. et al., Eds. *Italian Cultural Studies 2001*. Vol 33. Essays. $18

ELIZABETH G. MESSINA, Ed. *In Our Own Voices*. Vol 32. Italian/American
Studies. $25

STANISLAO G. PUGLIESE. *Desperate Inscriptions*. Vol 31. History. $12

HOSTERT & TAMBURRI, Eds. *Screening Ethnicity*. Vol 30. Italian/American
Culture. $25

G. PARATI & B. LAWTON, Eds. *Italian Cultural Studies*. Vol 29. Essays. $18

HELEN BAROLINI. *More Italian Hours*. Vol 28. Fiction. $16

FRANCO NASI, Ed. *Intorno alla Via Emilia*. Vol 27. Culture. $16

ARTHUR L. CLEMENTS. *The Book of Madness & Love*. Vol 26. Poetry. $10

JOHN CASEY, et al. *Imagining Humanity*. Vol 25. Interdisciplinary Studies. $18

ROBERT LIMA. *Sardinia/Sardegna*. Vol 24. Poetry. $10

DANIELA GIOSEFFI. *Going On*. Vol 23. Poetry. $10

ROSS TALARICO. *The Journey Home*. Vol 22. Poetry. $12

EMANUEL DI PASQUALE. *The Silver Lake Love Poems*. Vol 21. Poetry. $7

JOSEPH TUSIANI. *Ethnicity*. Vol 20. Poetry. $12

JENNIFER LAGIER. *Second Class Citizen*. Vol 19. Poetry. $8

FELIX STEFANILE. *The Country of Absence*. Vol 18. Poetry. $9

PHILIP CANNISTRARO. *Blackshirts*. Vol 17. History. $12

LUIGI RUSTICHELLI, Ed. *Seminario sul racconto*. Vol 16. Narrative. $10

LEWIS TURCO. *Shaking the Family Tree*. Vol 15. Memoirs. $9

LUIGI RUSTICHELLI, Ed. *Seminario sulla drammaturgia*. Vol 14. Theater/Essays. $10

FRED GARDAPHÈ. *Moustache Pete is Dead! Long Live Moustache Pete!*. Vol 13.
Oral Literature. $10

JONE GAILLARD CORSI. *Il libretto d'autore. 1860–1930*. Vol 12. Criticism. $17

HELEN BAROLINI. *Chiaroscuro: Essays of Identity*. Vol 11. Essays. $15

PICARAZZI & FEINSTEIN, Eds. *An African Harlequin in Milan*. Vol 10. Theater/
Essays. $15

JOSEPH RICAPITO. *Florentine Streets & Other Poems*. Vol 9. Poetry. $9

FRED MISURELLA. *Short Time*. Vol 8. Novella. $7

NED CONDINI. *Quartettsatz*. Vol 7. Poetry. $7

ANTHONY JULIAN TAMBURRI, Ed. *Fuori: Essays by Italian/American Lesbians
and Gays*. Vol 6. Essays. $10

ANTONIO GRAMSCI. P. Verdicchio. Trans. & Intro. *The Southern Question*. Vol 5.
Social Criticism. $5

DANIELA GIOSEFFI. *Word Wounds & Water Flowers*. Vol 4. Poetry. $8

WILEY FEINSTEIN. *Humility's Deceit: Calvino Reading Ariosto Reading Calvino*.
Vol 3. Criticism. $10

PAOLO A. GIORDANO, Ed. *Joseph Tusiani: Poet. Translator. Humanist*. Vol 2.
Criticism. $25

ROBERT VISCUSI. *Oration Upon the Most Recent Death of Christopher Columbus*.
Vol 1. Poetry.

CPSIA information can be obtained
at www.ICGtesting.com
Printed in the USA
BVOW03s0133200917
495387BV00001B/2/P

9 781599 541068